"When I Get Around To Kissing You, I'll Feel Better Knowing Your Mouth Doesn't Belong To Any Other Man. Legally Or Otherwise."

She didn't say anything for a moment. Then she opened her mouth, probably to tell him just where he could take his own mouth—legally or otherwise—but instead of saying anything right then, she just clamped her lips together.

He chuckled. "Tightening those lips shut won't keep me from a kiss, if that's what I want to do, Chloe."

Chloe folded her arms across her chest. "Is there a reason for this madness?"

"Is that what this is? Madness?" he asked.

She lifted her chin and glared at him. "You got another name for it?"

"What about *hunger?*"

Dear Reader,

Family is important to me and I love writing about the love and escapades that go on within the family structure. Can you imagine being in your middle twenties and helping a cousin barely a year older than you to raise your other young family members—all thirteen of them?

You've met Dillon Westmoreland in *Westmoreland's Way*. The second oldest of the Denver clan is Ramsey, a man who doesn't have marriage or love on his mind. Ramsey's only ambition is to make his sheep-ranching business a success. At least that was his only ambition until he met Chloe Burton. Now he's faced with something he thought could not happen to him, and that was the possibility of falling in love.

And Chloe has her own agenda, which doesn't include a serious involvement with Ramsey. She's done the *serious* thing with a man and it left her deciding it wasn't worth the trouble. Ramsey becomes a challenge to her peace of mind.

I hope that you find Ramsey and Chloe's story a very special one, and in the coming months I look forward to venturing into the lives of those other Westmorelands, as well.

Happy reading!

Brenda Jackson

BRENDA JACKSON

HOT WESTMORELAND NIGHTS

Published by Silhouette Books
America's Publisher of Contemporary Romance

To the love of my life, Gerald Jackson, Sr.

*To all the members of the Brenda Jackson Book Club. You are
a very special group and I appreciate each and every one of you!*

*To Val Manning of Rancho Terre Norte' in Colorado for assisting me with
my research on sheep ranching. You were simply wonderful!*

"Pleasant words are a honeycomb,
sweet to the soul and healing to the bones."
—Proverbs 16:24

SILHOUETTE BOOKS

ISBN-13: 978-0-373-73013-1

HOT WESTMORELAND NIGHTS

Copyright © 2010 by Brenda Streater Jackson

Recycling programs
for this product may
not exist in your area.

Printed in U.S.A.

BRENDA JACKSON

is a die "heart" romantic who married her childhood sweetheart and still proudly wears the "going steady" ring he gave her when she was fifteen. Because she's always believed in the power of love, Brenda's stories always have happy endings. In her real-life love story, Brenda and her husband of thirty-six years live in Jacksonville, Florida, and have two sons.

A *New York Times* bestselling author of more than fifty romance titles, Brenda is a recent retiree who worked thirty-seven years in management at a major insurance company. She divides her time between family, writing and traveling with Gerald. You may write Brenda at P.O. Box 28267, Jacksonville, Florida 32226, by e-mail at WriterBJackson@aol.com or visit her Web site at www.brendajackson.net.

THE DENVER WESTMORELAND FAMILY TREE

Raphel and Gemma Westmoreland

Stern Westmoreland (Paula Bailey)

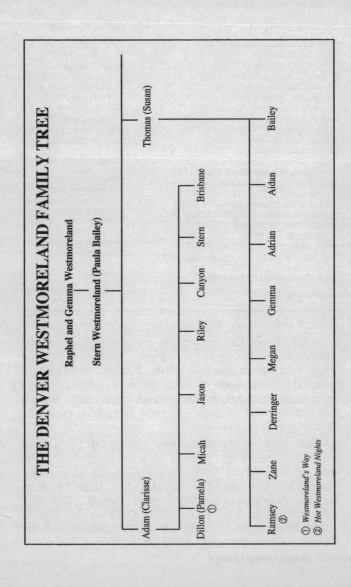

① *Westmoreland's Way*

② *Hot Westmoreland Nights*

Prologue

Chloe Burton pressed her face to the windowpane as she watched the man sprint across the street. Her heart began pounding in her chest. He had to be, without a doubt, the most handsome man she'd ever seen.

She stared as he stopped to talk to another man in front of a feed store. He was tall, dark and every inch of sexy from the Stetson he wore on his head to the well-worn leather boots on his feet. And from the way his jeans and western shirt fit his body, it was quite obvious he possessed powerful legs, strong arms, taut abs, tight buns and broad muscular shoulders. He had everything it took to separate the men from the boys.

And when he pushed back his hat, she saw dark eyes and a medium skin tone. Then she looked at his mouth and she couldn't help licking her lips at the sight of his. His lips were full, firm and luscious. She could imagine those lips and his mouth doing other things.

Just looking at him was enough to corrupt a woman's mind, she thought. Even from this distance, her body felt flushed, hot and unsettled. Nothing like this had ever happened to her while ogling a man in all her twenty-eight years.

Actually, over the past year the only male who had gotten her time and attention had been her *e-mail*. And that was mainly because her last relationship with Daren Fulbright had been totally unsatisfying, a complete waste of the year she'd put into it, and she was in no hurry to get into another. No doubt there were some who thought she'd given up on love much too quickly, and perhaps that was true since these days she much preferred curling up with a good book during her free time than with someone of the opposite sex. And now, here she was practically drooling at just the sight of a man. He might be major eye candy, but the man was a complete stranger to her. Even so, the way he was standing with both hands in his jeans pockets, legs braced apart, was a pose she would carry to her dreams.

And he was smiling, evidently enjoying his conversation. He had dimples, incredibly sexy dimples in not one but both cheeks.

"What are you staring at, Clo?"

Chloe nearly jumped. She'd forgotten she had a lunch date. In fact she had forgotten everything once her sights had landed on the sexy man across the street. She glanced over the table at her best friend from college, Lucia Conyers.

"Take a look at that man across the street in the blue shirt, Lucia, and tell me what you see. Would he not be perfect for Denver's first issue of *Simply Irresistible* or what?" Chloe asked with so much excitement in her voice she almost couldn't stand it.

Chloe was the owner of *Simply Irresistible,* a magazine for today's up-and-coming woman. The magazine had started out as a regional publication in the southeast, but had expanded to a national audience during the past few years. By far the magazine's most popular edition was the annual "Irresistible Man" issue. The feature included a cover shoot and an in-depth story on a man who the magazine felt deserved the honor because he was simply irresistible. As the magazine had expanded, Chloe had convinced Lucia to come on board to manage its Denver office.

When Lucia didn't say anything, Chloe's smile widened. "Well?"

Lucia glanced across the booth at her. "Since you asked, I'll tell you what I see. I see one of the Westmorelands, and in this case it's Ramsey Westmoreland. And to answer your other question as to whether he would be perfect for the cover man on *Simply Irresistible,* my answer would be a resounding yes, but he won't do it."

Chloe raised a brow. "I take it that you know him," she said watching her friend closely.

Lucia smiled. "Yes, but not as well as I know the younger Westmorelands. There's a lot of them and he's one of the oldest. I went to school with his younger siblings and cousins. He has several brothers and male cousins who look just as good. Maybe one of them will agree to do it, but you can forget Ramsey."

Chloe glanced back out the window and knew two things. First, there was no way that she could forget him. Second, from the sound of things it seemed that Lucia was interested in one of those "younger" male Westmorelands. She could hear the wistfulness in her friend's voice.

"He's the one I want, Lucia," she said with both determination and conviction in her voice. "And since you know him, then just ask him. He might surprise you and not turn you down. Of course he'll get paid for his services."

Lucia laughed and shook her head. "Getting paid isn't the issue, Clo. Ramsey is one of the wealthiest sheep ranchers in this part of Colorado. But everyone knows what a private person he is. Trust me, he won't do it."

Chloe hoped she was wrong. "But you will ask him?"

"Yes, but I suggest you move on and find another man."

Chloe glanced back out the window. The man was the epitome of what she was looking for in her "Irresistible Man" issue and she was determined to have him.

"Um, I don't like that look on your face, Chloe. I've seen it before and know exactly what it means."

Chloe couldn't help but smile. She could only blame her smile on her father, Senator Jamison Burton of Florida, the man who'd raised her alone after her mother died of cervical cancer when Chloe was three. Her father was the one man she most admired and he'd always taught her that if people wanted something bad enough, they wouldn't give up until they got it.

She glanced out the window and watched as Ramsey Westmoreland ended his conversation and entered the feed store with a swagger that almost made her breathless. She *would* be seeing him again.

One

"I can't believe you're not posing for the cover of that magazine, Ram."

Ramsey Westmoreland didn't bother to look up from arranging a bale of straw in the lambing stall. He'd figured his youngest sister Bailey would show up sooner or later, because news traveled pretty fast within the Westmoreland family. And of course, Bailey made it her life's work to know everything about her five brothers, down to their every heartbeat.

"I'm not going away, Ramsey, until you tell me what I want to know."

He couldn't help but smile at the threat because he knew if he gave her an order to leave that she *would* follow it. She might like to express her emotions and display her defiance every once in a while, and God help him when she did, but when it was all said and done, Bailey knew how far to take things with him. He would be the first to admit that she had tested his limits plenty, especially during those years when she and their cousin Bane had been almost inseparable. The two thought getting into trouble was a way of life.

Since then Bailey had finished high school and was now attending college, and Bane had surprised everyone with his decision last month to join the military with the goal of becoming a Navy Seal. All was quiet on the Westmoreland front and Ramsey would be the first to admit, but only to himself, things had been a little boring.

"There's nothing to tell," he decided to respond. "I was contacted about doing that cover and I turned them down."

"Just like that?"

"Just like that." He figured she was probably glaring at him right now.

"Why, Ram? Just think of the exposure."

He finally decided to look up and the gaze that sharpened on Bailey was so keen, had it been anyone else they would have had the good sense to take a step back. But not twenty-one-year-old Bailey Joleen Westmoreland. Of his three sisters—Megan, who was almost twenty-five and Gemma, who was twenty-three—Bailey was the boldest and could test the patience of Job, so to try the patience of her oldest brother was a piece of cake.

"I don't want exposure, Bailey. I think the Westmorelands got enough exposure all those years when we had to deal with the trouble you, Bane and the twins got into."

Not an ounce of regret flared in her eyes. "That was then. This is now. And this would have been good exposure."

He almost laughed at that one. "Good exposure for who exactly?" he asked, getting to his feet.

He had a lot to do and little time for chitchat. Nellie, who'd had the responsibility of preparing the meals for him and the ranch hands for the past two years, had to leave suddenly yesterday when she'd gotten word that her only sister back in Kansas had emergency surgery for a ruptured appendix. She intended to stay and help out and it would be at least two weeks before she returned.

Ramsey understood and supported her decision, although Nellie's absence left him in a bind. Today was the start of shearing and with over twenty or so men involved, he was in desperate need of a cook to take Nellie's place. He had placed a call to one of these temporary employment agencies yesterday afternoon and was told they had just the person who would be perfect as a fill-in and the woman was to show up this morning.

"It would be good exposure for you and the ranch. It could put you in the public eye and let everyone know how successful you are as a sheep rancher."

Ramsey shook his head. Being in the public eye was something he could definitely pass on. He was close to his family, but when it came to outsiders he was basically a loner and preferred things that way. Everyone knew how much he enjoyed his privacy. Bailey knew it too, so he wondered, why was she harassing him?

"The ranch doesn't need *that* kind of exposure. I was asked to pose for some girly magazine, Bail." He had never read a copy of *Simply Irresistible*, but the name alone made his jaw twitch. He could just imagine the articles that were between the covers.

"You should be flattered they want you on the cover, Ram."

He rolled his eyes. "Whatever." He then checked his watch for two reasons. This was Monday and he knew Bailey had a class at the university this morning *and* his temporary cook was ten minutes late.

"I wish you would reconsider."

He glanced back at her. "No," he said firmly. "And shouldn't you be in class about now?" He moved out of the barn and walked back toward the sprawling home he had finished building the previous year.

Bailey followed, right on his heels. He couldn't help but recall that she used to do that same thing when he took over the responsibility of raising her when she was seven and he was twenty-one. They'd lost both parents and a beloved aunt and uncle in an airplane accident. During that time she would rarely let him out of her sight. He fought back a smile at the fond memory.

"Yes, I have a class this morning, but I thought I'd drop by to talk some sense into you," he heard her say.

He turned around, placed his hands in his pockets. At that moment he couldn't stop the smile that touched his lips. "Fine. You've tried and failed. Goodbye, Bailey."

He watched her place her hands on her hips and lift her chin. No one had to warn him about Westmoreland stubbornness. Hers could be more lethal than most, but over the past twenty-one years he'd learned to deal with it.

"I think you're making a mistake. I subscribe to that magazine and I think you'd be surprised," she was saying. "It's not just a 'girly' magazine. It has a number of good articles for women, including some on health issues. However, once a year they feature a man on the cover. They try to find a man who's every woman's fantasy lover."

A woman's fantasy lover? Now that was a laugh, Ramsey thought. He was nothing more than a hardworking Colorado sheep rancher and since he'd doubled the size of his herd this past year, he couldn't recall the last time he'd been intimately involved with a woman. Working sunup to sundown, seven days a week had become a way of life for him.

"It will be my mistake to make, brat. I'll survive and so will you. Now scat."

A half-hour later he was alone and standing in his kitchen and clicking off his cell phone after talking to Colin Lawrence, a member of his shearing crew. Because of a snowstorm that had hit the area a few weeks ago, they were already behind in shearing and needed to get that done within the next two weeks in time for lambing to begin. Starting today everything would be moving rather fast to stay on schedule.

Colin had called to say a few of the pregnant ewes had somehow gotten out of the shearing pen and begun to wander. The dogs were having a hard time getting them back in the pen without stressing out the pregnant sheep. The last thing he needed was for any more shearing time to be lost, which meant that he had to get to the shearing plant on the north range as soon as possible.

He headed toward the door when he heard a car pull up outside. He glanced at his watch, agitated. It was about time the cook showed up. The woman was almost an hour late and that was not acceptable. And he intended to let her know about his displeasure.

Chloe brought the car to a stop in front of a huge two-story ranch-style structure and drew in a deep breath. She simply refused to take no for an answer regardless of what Ramsey Westmoreland had told Lucia. His refusal to be the cover story for her magazine was the reason she had ended a much-deserved vacation in the Bahamas to fly directly here. She intended to try to convince the man herself.

As she checked her GPS while traveling farther and farther

away from Denver's city limits and heading into a rural area the locals referred to as Westmoreland Country, she had asked herself why on earth would anyone want to live so far from civilization. That in itself was a mystery to her. She hadn't passed a single shopping mall along the way.

Looking out the car's window, she couldn't get out of her mind the man she had seen that day a couple of weeks ago. That was why she refused to move on and select someone else. The bottom line was that she didn't want anyone else. Ramsey Westmoreland was not only the man made for the title of *Simply Irresistible,* but he *was* simply irresistible.

Once she had turned off the main road, she saw the huge wooden marker that proudly proclaimed The Shady Tree Ranch. Beside it another smaller marker read *This is Westmoreland Country.* Lucia had said each of the fifteen Westmorelands owned a hundred acres of land where they had established their private residences. The main house sat on three hundred acres.

Once she turned off the main road, there had been several turnoffs, each denoted by smaller brick makers that indicated which Westmoreland the private driveway belonged to. She had traveled past Jason's Place, Zane's Hideout, Canyon's Bluff and Derringer's Dungeon before finally reaching Ramsey's Web.

She had done her research and knew everything she needed to know about Ramsey Westmoreland for now. He was thirty-six. A graduate of Tuskegee University's agricultural economics program, and had been in the sheep ranching business for about five years. Before that he and his cousin Dillon, who was older than Ramsey by only seven months, had run Blue Ridge Land Development, a multimillion-dollar company started by their fathers. Once the company had become successful Ramsey had turned the management of Blue Ridge over to Dillon to become the rancher he'd always wanted to be.

She also knew about the death of his parents and aunt and uncle in a car crash while Ramsey was in his final year of college. For the last fifteen years, Ramsey and Dillon had been responsible for their younger siblings. Dillon had gotten married three months ago, and he and his wife Pamela split their time between Dillon's home here and Pamela's home in a small town in Wyoming.

As far as Chloe was concerned, Ramsey Westmoreland was a success story and the type of man that women not only would want to fantasize about, but also one they would want to get to know in the article that would appear in her magazine.

She couldn't stop the fluttering in her stomach thinking that she was on property he owned and she would be seeing him again. If he had the ability to wreck her senses weeks after first setting eyes on him, she could just imagine what seeing him again would do. But she intended to handle herself as the professional that she was, while at the same time trying to convince him that sheep produced wool that eventually got weaved into articles of clothing—dresses, coats, jackets and such—that were mainly purchased by women.

She took another deep breath and opened the car door and got out at the same time the front door was slung opened and the man who'd tormented her dreams for the past couple of weeks stepped out on the porch with a scowl on his face, and said in a firm voice, "You are late."

Ramsey tried not to stare at the woman but couldn't help it. And this was supposed to be his temporary cook? She looked more like a model than a damn cook. There was no doubt in his mind that she would be able to generate plenty of heat in the kitchen or any other room she set foot in.

She was definitely a beauty with dark brown curly hair that flowed to her shoulders, dark brown eyes that looked seductive rather than contrite and a perfectly shaped mouth. And seeing her dressed in a pair of jeans that hugged her hips and pink blouse beneath a black leather jacket, made her look ultra-feminine and made him blatantly aware of his sexuality, while reminding him of just how long it had been since he'd been with a woman.

Ramsey hadn't expected this gut-stirring lust. He didn't need the attraction nor did he want it. It would be best for all concerned if she just got back in her car and returned to wherever she'd come from. But that wasn't possible. He had over twenty men to feed come lunchtime. He had managed to get through breakfast and thank goodness no one had complained. They had understood Nellie's emergency and had tolerated the slightly burned biscuits, scorched eggs and the overly crisp bacon. He had promised them a better meal for lunch. When they saw this woman they would definitely think *she* was a delicious treat.

"Excuse me. What did you say?"

He glanced across the yard where she was still standing by her car. Feeling frustrated as hell and fighting for control he walked down the steps, not taking his eyes off her. "I said you are late and your pay will be docked accordingly. The agency said you would be here at eight and it's now after nine. I have twenty men you'll need to feed at lunchtime. I hope there won't be a problem because I have plenty to do this morning and the agency assured me that you knew your way around a kitchen."

Chloe resisted the urge to ask what he was talking about.

Instead she spoke up and said, "Yes, I know my way around a kitchen."

"Then get to it. I'll be back for lunch and we can talk then, but I can tell you now that one of my pet peeves is tardiness," he said, moving toward his truck.

From what Chloe gathered he was expecting a cook who evidently was late in arriving. She should speak up now and explain to him that she was not the cook but he seemed to be in such a hurry. "Wait!"

He paused, turned sensual dark eyes on her and she felt a heated sensation rush up her spine at the same time she felt the tenderness in the nipples pressed against her blouse. "Look, lady, I don't have time to wait. I'm needed over at the shearing plant as we speak. You'll find everything you need in the kitchen."

His voice was hard, yet at the same time it sounded sexy. And she couldn't believe it when he hopped into his truck and pulled off. She couldn't do anything but stand there and watch him leave.

So much for having her say to convince him to do the magazine cover. For crying out loud, he thought she was a cook of all things. What she should do was to just get into her car and leave and come back another time, she thought. But where was this cook he was expecting? And did she hear him correctly when he said that come lunchtime there would twenty men to feed?

Chloe rubbed her hands down her face. Surely there was someone she could call who had his cell—who could get word to him of the grave mistake he'd made.

She turned toward the front door. He had left it wide open on the assumption that she would go inside, and at the moment she didn't have the common sense not to do so. If nothing else she could call Lucia. There was a chance Lucia knew how to contact a family member who would get word to him.

As Chloe walked up the steps it was easy to tell with the fresh-looking paint around the trim, white siding and brick sides that this was a relatively new house. There were a lot of windows facing the front, which provided a good view of the mountains and that were perfectly positioned to take advantage of the sunlight whenever it did appear, which wasn't too often this time of year. The porch wrapped around the front of the house, and the rocking chair and swing looked inviting enough to sit in the afternoons and just relax, even now in March when the weather was still cold.

And speaking of March weather, she tightened her jacket around her and walked into the living room, closed the door behind her and turned around. The place was huge and in the midst of the room, a spiral staircase led to the upstairs. There wasn't a whole lot of furniture in the room, but what was there looked rugged and sturdy. Few pictures hung on the wall and they were classic Norman Rockwell. The floor was hardwood with several area rugs scattered about.

She was about to walk through the living room to where she figured the kitchen was located when the phone rang. She quickly moved toward it, hoping it was either Ramsey Westmoreland or someone who knew how to reach him.

"Hello."

"This is Marie Dodson at the employment agency. May I speak with Mr. Ramsey Westmoreland, please?"

"He isn't here."

"Oh. Then please let him know there was a mix-up and the woman who was supposed to show up at his place this morning as a live-in cook for two weeks was sent somewhere else."

Chloe nodded and tapped her perfectly painted nail against the pad beside the phone. "All right, I'll be sure to tell him."

"He told me that his regular cook had to leave town unexpectedly due to a family emergency. I do hate leaving him in a bind like this with so many men to feed," the woman said with regret in her voice.

"I'm sure he will understand," was the only response Chloe felt she could make. "As a matter of fact, I think he's made other arrangements," Chloe added.

Moments later she was hanging up the phone, hoping that Ramsey Westmoreland *would* understand. But with what she guessed would be twenty hungry men come lunchtime, she wasn't so sure.

At that moment an idea flowed through her mind. Although her father had spoiled her rotten, he was a person who never forgot where he came from and believed in helping those less fortunate. That had been the main reason why she had spent her summers while home from college working at the homeless shelters. And since she enjoyed cooking, for three full summers while all her friends had spent time on the Florida beaches, she had volunteered her time helping out in the shelter's kitchens where large amounts of foods had to be cooked and served.

Mama Francine, who had worked as a cook at the shelter for years, had taught her all she needed to know, regardless of whether Chloe had wanted the education. Now it seemed all Mama Francine's cooking instructions about how to prepare food for a large group hadn't gone to waste.

Chloe tapped her finger to her chin. Maybe if she helped Ramsey Westmoreland out of this bind with lunch today, he just might be grateful enough to return the favor by doing her cover story. Especially if she made sure he felt he owed her big time. She smiled, liking the thought of that.

After glancing at her watch she took off her jacket and rolled up her sleeves as she headed toward the kitchen. One good favor deserved another and she was counting on Ramsey Westmoreland seeing things that way.

TWO

Ramsey's jaw tightened as he slowed his truck to a stop. He had been in such a hurry to get out of the woman's presence that he hadn't taken time to even ask for her name. All he could think about was how his testosterone level had suddenly kicked into gear and that a sexual hunger, unlike any he'd ever experienced before, had begun sliding up his spine.

And the woman was his cook? A live-in cook for two weeks? How in the hell was he supposed to handle something like that? He couldn't imagine sharing space of any kind with her. There was something about her that drew him, made him think of things he hadn't thought of in a long time, had no business thinking about now. Lustful things.

Crap!

He slid the truck into gear to start moving again. What he should do is to turn around, go back and tell her as nicely as he could that she wouldn't work out. Then he'd call the employment agency and request that they send out a replacement.

He checked his watch, wondering how much time it would take to get another cook out to his place. Would the agency be able to find someone else right away? At least in time for lunch? Probably not, which meant he was stuck with the woman at least through today. But what if the agency couldn't find anyone else by tomorrow? What then?

He brought the truck to another stop and rubbed his hand down his face. This wasn't good. The shearers had been at it since six that morning after eating the pitiful breakfast that he had prepared. And he of all people knew his men worked hard and expected a good meal at lunch to keep going until the end of the day. And as their employer it was his job to make sure they got it.

As he turned his truck toward the area where the shearing plant was located he set his jaw in determination as he thought about the challenges that lay ahead with his new cook. He grabbed his cell phone off the seat beside him and figured that maybe he should call the house and check on her, make sure things were running smoothly, and then he quickly decided against it. Although he hadn't given the woman time to say much of anything, he had liked the sound that had flowed from her lips with the few words that she'd spoken.

She looked young, maybe a year or two older than his sister Megan who would be turning twenty-five in a few months. Why would a woman that young want to be a ranch cook? The scowl on his face deepened. Sniffing behind any woman was something he hadn't done in a long time and was something he wouldn't be doing now.

A satisfied smile touched Chloe's face as she glanced around the huge kitchen thinking she had somehow pulled it off. Granted she'd had to call Mama Francine and the older woman had walked her through the peach cobbler recipe, but once Chloe had begun moving around, getting familiar with her surroundings, she had felt within her element. She had made herself at home. She enjoyed cooking, although she would prefer not doing so on a constant basis for a small army.

Ramsey Westmoreland had a well-equipped kitchen with beautiful granite countertops and a number of shining stainless steel pots hanging from a rack. There was an industrial-size refrigerator, a large stove and a spacious walk-in pantry filled to capacity and in neat order. She had been able to find everything she had needed without any problems.

She had glanced through the cook's log that was kept on the kitchen counter. She saw that on most Mondays the men were fed chicken and dumplings, string beans and bread pudding for lunch. To Chloe's way of thinking that menu sounded bland and she had a mind to fix something different. She'd decided on lasagna, a tossed salad and Texas toast. For dessert she figured the peach cobbler would do the trick.

And she had set the table differently. Although she figured when it was time to eat a hungry man didn't care how the table looked, she decided to spruce things up with a different tablecloth, a springy yellow instead of the plaid one that had been on the table and appeared to have seen better days.

It seems that knowing he would always feed a huge work crew, Mr. Westmoreland had built a spacious banquet-size dining room off from the eat-in kitchen with tables and chairs to comfortably accommodate around fifty people. To her way of thinking, it was a smart move and showed just how much he cared for his employees. They would feel important enough to eat under the boss's roof instead of them being relegated to eating in the bunkhouse. To her that said a lot about the kind of employer he was.

She checked her watch. With less than fifteen minutes left she figured it was time to place the serving dishes on the table when she heard a vehicle pull up outside. She glanced out the window and saw it was the truck Ramsey Westmoreland had been driving that morning.

She stiffened, then drew in a deep breath, fighting for control and refusing to come unglued. No matter how handsome the man was, the only thing she wanted was for him to agree to do her magazine cover. She glanced out the window and saw he hadn't gotten out the truck yet and figured because he had arrived that his men were probably not too far behind.

With that thought in mind she moved to the stove to go about getting everything prepared.

Ramsey leaned back in the leather seat and stared at his house, not sure if he was ready to get out of the truck and go inside. He sniffed the air and then out of curiosity he rolled down the window.

Was that something Italian? He inhaled sharply thinking that it certainly smelled like it. When was the last time he and his men had something besides chicken and dumplings on Monday? Nellie was a fantastic cook, but she detested change. When it came to lunch his men could expect chicken and dumplings on Monday, shepherd's pie on Tuesday, chili on Wednesday, beef stew on Thursday and baked chicken on Friday. Nellie was known to keep things simple.

Deciding he couldn't sit in his truck forever, he opened the door to get out. By the time he rounded the front of his truck his front door opened. He stopped walking, literally froze in his tracks as he stared at the woman who stepped out on the porch.

His eyes hadn't played tricks on him that morning. She was a pleasant sight for the sorest of eyes and so stunningly beautiful that he felt every male hormone inside his body shift into overdrive. He struggled, unsuccessfully, to control the attraction he felt toward her. But when a knot twisted in his stomach, he knew he had to get her gone and off his property as soon as reasonably possible. Her being here for any amount of time was not going to work.

Chloe was going through her own issues as she studied the fierce frown on Ramsey Westmoreland's face. She wondered what had him so uptight. She had been the one who'd spent the last two hours in the kitchen over a hot stove, so she saw no reason for what she perceived as an unpleasant demeanor. If he knew the real deal and how she had helped him out of a sticky situation he would be kissing her feet.

And speaking of kissing her feet…

Her mind paused, got stuck on that thought as a vision played out in her head of his actually kissing her feet before his mouth traveled upward to tackle other parts of her body. The very idea made her tighten her hands into fists at her sides at the same time a wave of heated desire suffused her senses.

Jeez. She had been dealing with all kinds of emotions and sensations since entering the man's home, and for her misery he owed her big time.

Yet at the moment, Ramsey Westmoreland was more than a little intimidating. Chloe wasn't sure if she wanted this man indebted to her in any way. He had the look of a man who shared humor only when it suited him. A man who wouldn't hesitate to offer his opinions and not necessarily in a tactful way. He would tell you exactly what he thought. And she had a feeling that he was not a man who made foolish mistakes, or one who could easily be led around by a woman. The latter perversely bothered her because she was used to being in total control of any relationships she got involved in. But then, she and this man were not involved.

Deciding they had wasted enough time sizing up each other, she spoke up. "You were in such a hurry to leave this morning that I didn't get a chance to introduce myself. I'm Chloe Burton."

"You were late this morning."

She couldn't help the frown that settled on her face. Was he thinking of reminding her of it at every turn? Evidently he had very little tolerance for certain things. "No one told me that once I left Denver's city limits that I would be headed for the boondocks, away from normal civilization. You're lucky I made it here at all. So the way I see it is you really should be counting your blessings, Mr. Westmoreland."

Chloe could tell by the way his brow lifted that he was somewhat surprised by her flippant tone. She noted his rigid stance and drew in a fortifying breath, thinking he really shouldn't be so uptight. Life was serious, but there was no reason to take it to the edge. Her father had been that way until a heart attack brought on by stress had nearly done him in a few years ago.

"So when can I expect the other men? I made a feast," she said, deciding to change the subject.

His gaze narrowed at her with shimmering intensity. "They'll finish up and should be here any minute, so we need to talk before they arrive."

Chloe decided then and there that she didn't want to talk. His voice was just like the rest of him, sexy as hell. There was richness to his Western accent that caused a tightness in her throat. Being in his presence for the past few moments had frazzled her nerves, had blood pounding through her veins and had unceremoniously reminded her of the hormones he'd awakened since the first time she had set eyes on him. It also stirred warm emotions, confusing feelings she hadn't felt in a while...if ever. That was not good.

"What do we have to talk about? You've made it clear I was late and my pay would be docked. What else are you out for? Blood?"

Ramsey tensed. Evidently at some point the woman had forgotten that she was the employee and he the employer. Maybe her past employers found her attitude amusing, but he didn't. He opened his mouth to state such a thing, but closed it when he heard the trucks pull up, which signaled the arrival of his men.

"We'll have to wait and talk after lunch," he said tersely. And then without saying anything else, he turned and headed toward the bunkhouse to wash up for lunch.

Ramsey leaned back in his chair thinking he had eaten lasagna before but never this delicious. And from glancing around the room at his men, he figured they were thinking the same thing. And there had been more than enough, which was a good thing because a number of the men had asked for seconds.

And he hadn't been able not to notice that he wasn't the only one who enjoyed seeing Ms. Burton work the room as she made sure everyone had everything they needed. Initially he'd been amused when the guys first arrived and a number of them, once they'd noticed there wasn't a ring on her finger, had tried their hand at flirting. But she had maintained a degree of professionalism that had impressed him. Even Eric Boston and

Thelon Hinton, the two hard-core womanizers in the group, had pretty much backed off when it became obvious that she wasn't returning their interest. That surprised him because those two had a reputation in Denver of being sought-after ladies' men.

Another thing that had impressed him about Chloe Burton was the way she had set up the employee dining room. It was obvious she had taken the time to spruce things up a bit, changing the decor of the men's surroundings. Changing the menu had also been a plus.

He had good men who worked hard. Moreover, they would be putting in long hours during the next two weeks. Most had been with him since he'd started the operation and were family men who went home for dinner and returned for work each day. After shearing, which occurred once a year, some of his men would turn their attention to lambing, while the others would resume their roles as sheepherders.

"I see you can't keep your eyes off her either, Ram."

Ramsey shot a sharp glance over at Callum Austell. When Ramsey had decided to become a sheep rancher he had flown over to Australia to spend six months on one of the country's largest sheep ranches. It was there that he'd met the Aussie, who happened to be the youngest son of the ranch owner. Callum had agreed to come to the States to help Ramsey start his operation. Now three years later, Callum was still here with him. He was the one who'd basically taught Ramsey everything he knew about sheep. He considered Callum a good friend.

"You must be seeing things, Aussie," was Ramsey's reply, even though he knew Callum was right. Okay, so he was looking at her, but because he was her employer he needed to make sure she did her job right and that she conducted herself properly. He had twenty-five employees year round and not including Nellie, they were all men. And he was a hands-on boss, so he was familiar with everything that went on with his ranch and if needed, he could fill in for any of his men.

"I think not, but if you want to convince yourself of it, then go ahead," was Callum's comeback. "All I got to say is that you should be impressed with the way she handled Eric and Thel. I think she might have broken their hearts."

Ramsey couldn't help but snort at that. If that was true, it was about time some woman did. He glanced down at his watch. Lunch was almost over and the men, knowing his policy about punctuality, were standing to leave and were giving Chloe Burton all kinds of compliments. He stood as well, but unlike his men he had no intentions of going anywhere until he had a talk with his cook.

After grabbing his hat off the hat rack, Callum rounded the table and halted in front of Ramsey and studied his features. "I hope you don't plan on ruining things for the rest of us. We like her cooking. And we like her. We would like to keep her around, at least until Nellie comes back."

Callum had quietly spoken his words, just for Ramsey's benefit. Without glancing over at Callum, Ramsey said, "We'll see."

And for now that was all he would say on the matter. Yes, the woman had impressed him and his men with her cooking skills, and yes, she had carried herself in a professional way. But Callum had been right. Just like his men he hadn't been able to stop looking at her and that wasn't a good thing. He had been sitting at the table eating his lasagna and imagining eating her instead. His mind was so filled with lust it wasn't funny, and the flame that burned deep inside him wasn't amusing, either.

He glanced over his shoulder and saw the last of the men had gone, all but Callum, who threw him a daggered look before walking out the door and closing it behind him. Ramsey pulled in a deep, frustrated breath. The impression Chloe had already made on his men was not a good thing. Even if she stayed for two weeks she would have to leave when Nellie returned anyway.

He heard the rattling of the dishes and glanced over at Chloe, watching her as she cleared the table. His gaze slowly swept over her figure, liking the way the jeans fit across her backside. He figured her height was probably around five-eight and he would bet all the wool his sheep would be producing this year that she had long beautiful legs. The kind that would be a killer pair in a miniskirt.

He shook his head thinking about his fetish for seeing women in short skirts. He was a leg man all the way. So why was seeing this woman in jeans having basically the same effect?

Really it didn't matter because he planned to let her go as soon as he could get in a replacement. Temptation was temptation and he would hate to suddenly develop sleepwalking tendencies knowing she would be in the guest bedroom down the hall from him.

Hell, such a thought no matter how tempting, didn't sit well with him, mainly because he made the Double Creek Sheep Ranch one of the most successful in the United States. He'd done so by staying focused on what needed to be done and not by getting caught up in a woman. He didn't intend to get caught up on one now.

He leaned against the counter, deciding not to interrupt what she was doing just yet. Not when he had her within his scope. Whether he liked it, he was enjoying the view.

* * *

The man was agitated about something, Chloe could sense it, but at the moment she refused to let him get on her last nerve. She had plenty of work to do and didn't have time for a confrontation. After she was finished clearing the table she would break the news to Mr. Westmoreland that she was not his cook, that she had done him a favor and that she expected one in return.

The room was quiet, but she could hear his breathing, strong and steady. But even though she refused to look over at him, she was well aware he was looking at her, checking her out. And she knew he was paying a lot of attention to her backside, probably had his gaze locked on it real tight, which would account for the heat she actually felt on that part of her anatomy. She'd been told by more than one man that she had a nice derriere, curvy and shapely, just the way a man liked. *Whoopie,* she thought sarcastically.

But still, she would be the first to admit that just the thought that Ramsey Westmoreland's gaze was on her bottom almost made her breath catch in her throat. His eyes, whenever she looked into them, were filled with intensity and she could actually feel that intensity now focused directly on her.

Not able to stand it a minute longer, she swung around and frowned deeply. "We can talk now."

His dark eyes remained steady on her, even when he nodded and said, "All right. First I want to say you did a heck of a job with lunch today. The men were impressed and so was I."

She blinked. A compliment hadn't been what she'd been expecting. The man definitely had a way of delivering it with mixed emotions. His words were syrupy and sweet, while the texture of his voice was brooding. "Thank you, I'm glad everyone enjoyed it."

"They also enjoyed you." At the lift of her brow he clarified and said, "Enjoyed you being here I mean."

She wondered where he was about to go with that comment and figured she would know soon enough. "I enjoyed being here as well," she responded as she placed the dishes in the sink. It was time to come clean and let him know her real purpose for being there. "Mr. Westmoreland, I think that you—"

"Ramsey. I prefer you call me Ramsey. Everyone around here does. Some even call me Ram."

She couldn't help but smile at that.

"You find something amusing, Ms. Burton?"

She met his gaze and her smile widened even more. "You can call me Chloe, and what I find amusing is the fact that a ram is a male sheep and you are in the sheep business. Unique, don't you think?"

He shrugged muscular shoulders. "Never gave it much thought."

She lifted a brow. "Are you trying to tell me that no one has ever made the connection before?"

"If they did, they knew better than to mention it."

Chloe wanted to just throw her hands up in the air and give up. It was quite evident that even when they were trying to hold a civil conversation they had the ability to rub each other the wrong way. That made her wonder about him, the man she wanted to be on the cover of *Simply Irresistible*. He looked better than chocolate cake oozing with deep, rich chocolate icing—her favorite—but it was becoming quite evident he was a complex man. She couldn't help wonder what made Ramsey tick? What would it take to make him become relaxed, more laid-back? she wondered. Although she could see that around his men he was pretty mild-mannered and friendly. It was obvious they had a good working relationship while maintaining a degree of respect. That meant he was reserving his uptightness mainly for her. She wondered why.

The research she'd done indicated he dated when the mood or the urge probably hit him. Yet he didn't have any steady woman in his life. His last serious relationship had been with the woman he'd become engaged to, a woman by the name of Danielle McKay. However, she had ruined what was to have been his wedding day by stopping the minister in the middle of the wedding and walking out. That had been over ten years ago. Surely he'd gotten over that incident by now.

In addition to the cover photo for the magazine, she wanted an interview with him and had a feeling getting him to talk would be just as difficult as getting him to agree to the cover photo. Talk about pulling teeth. She had planned to send one of her seasoned reporters to talk to him and now she could clearly see that just wouldn't work.

Suddenly an idea popped into her head. She might as well go about killing two birds with one stone. She wanted him to do the magazine cover and she wanted an article on him as well. His profession intrigued her. For instance, why had he gotten into sheep ranching versus cattle or horse ranching?

An insider's view of his operation might be good reading information to her readers. And the best way to find out everything she wanted to know about him was to hang around and get to know him for herself. The man was without a doubt masculine perfection and she wondered if there was more to Ramsey Westmoreland than a handsome face and a hard, muscular body.

Chloe nibbled on her lower lip. Now was the time to come clean and tell him the truth, but something was holding her back from doing so. He owed her for lunch today and she intended to collect, but she wanted more from him than just the photo cover. She wanted to interview him for a piece in the magazine as well. Women loved wool and she could do an article informing them of the entire process of getting it off the sheep and into the stores. At lunch a number of the shearers had explained how things were done, but she wanted to hear it from Ramsey.

"What made you get into sheep ranching?" she decided to ask. There was no sense in wasting time getting the information she needed.

She glanced over at him when he didn't say anything and felt heat thrum through her body when he shifted his gaze to her face. From his expression she could tell he was surprised by her question.

"Why do you want to know?"

He was a suspicious sort and she would add that to the list of his characteristics. "I'm just curious. You have a big spread and a good number of men to help you run things. Most people around here have cattle or horses, but you have sheep. Why?"

Taking his time, Ramsey pondered Chloe's question. It was one he had asked himself many times and whenever he did he would always come up with the same answer. "Being a rancher was a dream my father and I shared from the time he took me with him to visit a friend of his in Maryland who owned a sheep farm. I couldn't have been any more than twelve at the time. In college I majored in agriculture economics, so I would know everything there was to know about farming and ranching, although my plans were to join the family's real estate business like everyone else. It was Dad's intent to one day retire and just have a small flock of sheep, but he died before he had a chance to fulfill his dream."

"I'm sorry, Ramsey."

She had spoken quietly and he saw his sorrow reflected in her eyes. He quickly wondered why he had shared that with her. He wasn't sure why he had answered her question at all. What was it about her that had made him feel comfortable enough with her to bare his soul? "Look, Chloe, what I need to talk to you about is—"

At that moment his cell phone went off. "Excuse me," he said before fishing it out of his back pocket. "Yes?"

She watched, nearly mesmerized as a huge smile touched his face, curving his lips. If she hadn't seen it, she would not have believed it. Did he reserve his frowns just for her?

"Dillon, when did you get in?" He paused. "No problem, I'm on my way."

He quickly returned the phone to his jeans pocket and glanced over at her. "I need to run. We still need to talk. I'll be back in an hour or so." He turned to move toward the back door.

"I'll be gone by then."

He stopped and pivoted around and lifted a questioning brow while staring at her. "Gone where?"

There were those intense eyes again and she drew a breath. "Back to town."

He leaned back against the counter again. "Did the agency not tell you that I hired you as a live-in cook? The men will be expecting another meal in the morning around five."

"Five!"

"Yes."

She looked at him suspiciously. "Did your other cook live here?"

"No. But then I didn't have to worry about her getting here early enough to have breakfast ready for my men. Nellie and her husband have a house less than ten miles away. She arrived every morning at three and left in the late afternoon."

He then lifted a brow. "Just what did that employment agency tell you? This is shearing time here at the ranch and it happens only once a year. I own over three thousand sheep and have only a two-week window to get the wool off. Unlike a lot of sheep ranchers who hire a sheep shearing crew from year to year, my men are trained to do all the job duties here. That means they will work around the clock. I have to make sure they eat a hearty breakfast and are fed a good lunch. I can't wake up tomorrow morning and worry about whether you'll show up."

"I'll be back in the morning," she heard herself say. "I promise."

Ramsey frowned. Hadn't he made up his mind that they could not stay under the same roof? Wasn't it his intent to talk to her about remaining as his cook only until he'd found a replacement? So why was he making a big deal of her staying over tonight? He should be overjoyed that she was leaving.

He inwardly shrugged and figured he only cared because of his concern that she would not be here on time in the morning to feed his men. "I'm going to need you here on time, Chloe," he said in a voice that sounded pretty damn curt even to his own ears.

"I said I would be here, didn't I?" she all but snapped back in a tone that said he would get just as good as he gave.

His glare locked on her face and then he nodded stiffly. "I'm taking you at your word. Lock the door behind you when you leave and I'll see you in the morning." He then headed for the door.

He turned and met her gaze one more time and she didn't release her breath until the door had closed behind him.

Three

"Please tell me you're joking, Clo."

Chloe sat her luggage down near her feet and turned to Lucia who had a worried look on her face. Chloe had decided to return to Ramsey's place tonight instead of trying to find her way there again in the early morning when it would still be dark outside. "Come on, Lou, it's not that serious. I'm doing Ramsey Westmoreland a favor and in the end he will be doing me a favor."

Lucia rolled her eyes. "He won't see things that way when he finds out what you're really about. You're not only invading his privacy, but you're also being deceitful."

"I'm not."

"You are, too, and all hell is going to break loose when he learns the truth. I live in this town, you don't. You'll be back in sunny Florida and I'll be here feeling the heat of the

Westmorelands' wrath. When it comes to anyone messing with one of them, they all stick together."

Chloe crossed her arms beneath her breasts and gave her best friend a pointed look. "And which Westmoreland are you concerned with pissing off, Lucia?"

Chloe knew she had hit the jackpot when Lucia dropped her gaze and began looking everywhere but at her. "I don't know what you're talking about."

Chloe had no intentions of believing that. "Yeah, right. You don't want to make waves with the Westmorelands for a reason, so fess up. Which one is it? Ramsey?"

"No," Lucia said quickly. "It's no one."

Chloe didn't believe that any more than she believed there was a lost colony off the California coast. "Okay, Lou, this is Clo. You can't lie straight even on your best days, so I'm going to ask you one more time, who is he and don't waste my time telling me he's not a Westmoreland."

Reluctantly, Lucia met her gaze and then in a quiet and flat voice she said, "It's Ramsey's brother, Derringer."

Chloe raised a brow. Her best friend's expression was filled with so much love it almost hurt her to look at it. "Derringer Westmoreland? When did all this take place?"

She had known Lucia since her first year of college and the man's name had never come up, yet judging by the expression on Lucia's face whatever she felt for the man ran deep and had been there a long time.

A faint smile touched Lucia's lips. "I've loved him forever."

Chloe was shocked. "Forever? And I'm just hearing about him?"

Lucia shrugged. "There was never a point. My crush began in high school, but he saw me as nothing more than one of his sister's friends. I thought I'd gotten over him when I left for college but since returning home four years ago I've discovered that isn't the case."

Lucia's face warmed when she said, "Last month I ran into him, and for the first time in years we were close enough to speak." A smile then touched her face. "And he asked me—"

"Out on a date?" Chloe asked excitedly.

"I wish. He dropped by my dad's paint store and I was working behind the counter and Derringer asked me to hand him a can of paint thinner."

Chloe couldn't help the grin that curved her lips. Evidently that little incident had made Lou's day. Just being around Ramsey Westmoreland put a spark in *her* day. Now where had that thought come from? Chloe wondered.

"Now that I know how you feel about Derringer Westmoreland, I will tell Ramsey the truth as soon as reasonably possible. I still want to make him feel indebted to me first for a while and then I'll level with him and come clean."

Lucia nodded. "I know how much having Ramsey on the cover of your magazine as well as doing that article on him means to you."

Chloe met Lucia's gaze and smiled. "Yes, I don't want you to worry about it because I believe in the end we'll both get what we want."

Ramsey looked up from the breeding charts he had spread over his desk and considered going into the kitchen to eat that last bit of peach cobbler that had been left from lunch. It had been so delicious his mouth was beginning to water just thinking about it.

And his mouth was beginning to water just thinking about

something else as well. More specifically, someone else. Chloe Burton. Talk about looking yummy. He threw his pencil down and leaned back in his chair. At that moment he couldn't help but think about snug-fitting jeans that covered a curvaceous backside and a blouse that fit perfectly over a tempting pair of breasts. He was getting aroused at the memory.

Damn.

Deciding he needed a beer more so than any peach cobbler, he got up to make his way to the kitchen. Moments later he was leaning against the counter and tipping the bottle to his lips and taking a much-needed drink. Lowering the bottle he then glanced around the room and for the first time noticed just how large and quiet his home was. Usually he welcomed the silence, but for some reason it bothered him tonight.

He studied the ceramic floor as he thought about his great-grandfather, Raphael Westmoreland, who had owned over eighteen hundred acres of land on the outskirts of Denver's city limits. When each Westmoreland reached the age of twenty-five they were given a one-hundred-acre tract of land. It was why he, his siblings and cousins all lived in close proximity to each other. As the oldest cousin, in addition to receiving his one hundred acres, Dillon had also inherited Shady Tree Ranch, the Westmoreland family home. The huge two-story dwelling sat on three hundred acres and hosted the majority of the family functions. Since Dillon had married Pamela it seemed the Westmorelands had reason to celebrate a lot. Everyone adored Dillon's wife, found her totally different from his first wife, and had welcomed Pamela and her three sisters into the family with open arms.

He lifted his head when he heard a knock at his door and glanced up at the clock on the wall. It was close to eleven, but that didn't mean a damn thing to any of his siblings or cousins. They felt they had a right to come calling at any time. He shook his head as he made it to the door, thinking it was probably his sister Megan. She was twenty-four years old and an anesthesiologist at the hospital in town.

Without bothering to ask who it was, he slung his front door open to find Chloe Burton standing on his porch and tightly gripping a piece of luggage. He was so surprised to see her that he could only stand and stare.

He could tell by the way she was nibbling on her lower lip that she was nervous, but that wasn't what held his attention, although the action caused a tightening in his gut. What had him transfixed was her outfit. She had almost ruined a saucy minidress by wearing leggings. He would have loved to see her bare legs and almost sighed in disappointment. But then he had to admit she still looked gorgeous and sexy as hell. Good enough to eat after first lapping her all over. He swallowed knowing at that moment that he was in trouble.

"I know I said I'd come back in the morning, but I figured not to take any chances getting here late. Besides, I need to get things set up, if the men eat at five. I'll need to be in the kitchen at least by four. So…here I am."

Yes, here she was, and although he wished otherwise, ideas continued to pop up in his head, literally pound his brain, regarding all the things he'd like to do to her. Even now he wished like hell he could ignore the ache that was stirring in the lower part of his body, as well as the heavy thudding doing havoc to his chest. But he couldn't.

She stared at him and he stared back at her as his insides began filling with lust of the thickest kind. He should have followed his mind earlier and contacted the employment agency to see if they could send in a replacement by morning, but he had failed to do so mainly because deep down he really hadn't wanted to. He grudgingly admitted that he had been looking forward to seeing her in the morning. But she was here now and he wasn't quite sure just how to handle her unexpected arrival.

He watched as she raised her brows. "So are you going to let me in or do I get to stand out here all night?"

At that moment he couldn't help but quirk his lips in a smile. She was almost as bad as Bailey with her sassy mouth. A mouth that at that moment snagged his gaze. Breath slammed through his lungs when she took that time to moisten her lower lip with the tip of her tongue.

He fought the heat flaring in his midsection. "Yes, I'm going to let you in," he said, reaching out and taking the luggage out of her hand and stepping back and moving aside.

"I appreciate it," she responded, stepping over the threshold.

When she walked past him every cell in Ramsey's body began throbbing as he took in her scent. Whatever perfume she was wearing was lethal and could wrap a man up in all kinds of sensuous thoughts.

She glanced over at him. "So where's my room?"

He gave her a tight smile. "Upstairs. Please follow me." A part of him wished he was leading her to his bedroom instead of the guest room. Damn, he needed another beer.

They walked up the stairs and when they reached the landing they walked down the hall. "Nice place."

He glanced over his shoulder. "I'm sure you've seen it before."

She arched her brow. "No, I haven't. Earlier today when you left your door wide open, I had no reason to snoop around up here. My job was in the kitchen area and no other part of your house."

He wondered if she could be believed, and when he glanced over his shoulder again he couldn't help but note how she was checking out several of the bedrooms they passed. Maybe she hadn't come *snooping* after all. He had five guest rooms all with their own private baths. At twenty-three, Gemma was the interior designer in the family. She had been more than happy to spend his money to lavishly decorate each of his bedrooms. And she was dying to get started on the rooms downstairs once he gave her the go-ahead. That wouldn't be for a while. He was still recovering from having her underfoot when she'd done the upstairs.

"Sorry, my mistake," he apologized by saying.

When they reached the bedroom that she would be using, he stood back to let her enter. He could tell from her expression that he had made a wise choice. She liked it, which meant she was a frilly, lacy and soft colors kind of girl. While she was standing in the middle of the room, scanning the room in awe, he placed her luggage on the bed.

His first inclination was to bid her good-night and leave her standing right there, but something about the expression on her face stopped him. She actually seemed absorbed. He somehow understood. Gemma's interior design work could do that to you. He would be one of the first to admit that his sister was good. The money used to send her to college had been well spent.

He doubted there was ever a time Gemma hadn't wanted to be an interior designer. He could vividly recall how she had made curtains for his first car—a bright red Chevy—when she was eight. To not hurt her feelings he had mounted the things in the car's rear window hoping that none of his friends saw them.

"Whoever decorated this part of your home did a fantastic job," Chloe said, as her gaze returned to Ramsey.

Chloe noted that he was looking at her again, with the same intensity that he'd looked at her earlier that day. And as she stared back his gaze never wavered, it held hers deep within its scope. Without words, with barely a breath, something was taking place between them. She wished she could dismiss her theory and believe she was just imagining things, but there was no make-believe with the heat consuming her body. Her breasts suddenly felt swollen and her nipples seemed tender against the fabric of her dress.

Her gaze moved from his face and scanned his body downward and was glad to see she was not the only one affected by the moment. He was aroused. Fully. There was no way he could hide it and he wasn't trying to. Her gaze shifted back to his face and what she saw in the depths of his eyes almost took her breath away. There were promises of hot, lusty nights, more pleasure than she could probably stand, kisses that would start at her mouth and end between her thighs and an explosion that would shatter every single thing within her. She paused for breath at the thought that those were real promises she saw in his gaze and not a figment of her imagination.

Then she also saw something else in the depths of his eyes beside those promises. She saw a warning. If she couldn't stand the heat, then she needed to stay out of the kitchen. At that moment she pulled in a wary breath. Was Ramsey Westmoreland the one man she could not handle?

"I'll leave you alone to unpack," he finally said, breaking the intense sexual tension that surrounded them. "You have your own bathroom, which I believe you'll find more than sufficient."

She nodded. Her ability to speak had escaped her.

"Good night, Chloe. I'll see you in the morning."

She could only stand and stare after him as he left the room.

There was no doubt about it. He had to get her out of his house, Ramsey thought, as he paced his bedroom hours later. What had happened in the guest room tonight was uncalled for, but still pretty much unclear. He had come within seconds of crossing that room, bending his head and taking her mouth with his to satisfy the hunger he felt. The hunger he was still feeling. The thought of his tongue mingling with hers while he held her tight against the heat of his chest caused the hot stab of arousal to nearly knock him to his knees.

And where on earth had such passion come from? It had nearly taken over him, transformed his brains into mush and had filled his mind with naughty thoughts of all the things he wanted to do to her. He pulled in a deep breath deciding he needed to analyze the situation. He needed to determine just how they had come to this point.

He would be the first to admit there had been a strong sexual attraction from the first moment he'd laid eyes on her. A rush of hot blood had shot through his veins, had hammered away at his insides, and an awareness as profound as anything he'd ever encountered before had zinged through him with the force of a volcano erupting. Every nerve, every bone and every muscle in his body had been affected.

And things hadn't gotten any better during the lunch hour when he hadn't been able to keep his eyes off her just as Callum had claimed. And he had a feeling that the reason Eric and Thel had probably backed off hadn't been because of any feeling of defeat where she was concerned. They had retreated because they'd picked up on his interest. If Callum had noticed

his staring at her, then there was a strong possibility others
had as well. And because doing such a thing was so unlike
him, they probably figured he was being territorial. Had he
been?

He rubbed his hands down his face as he uttered a frustrated
curse. She was probably in her bed, sleeping peacefully
between the sheets, while he was the one walking the floor
with an erection that was keeping him awake. He seriously
considered going into her room, getting her up and asking her
to leave. How crazy was that? To even contemplate doing such
a thing showed just how close to the edge he was.

Of his four brothers he was the one who could generally
take a woman or leave her just where she stood. His love 'em
and leave 'em attitude unnerved his siblings who thought he
spent more time sleeping with his sheep than with women.
Considering the time he'd done duty as a sheepherder over
the past year, that accusation was not a lie. But it really wasn't
any of their business. And he had been quick to point out—
especially to his brothers and male cousins—that they were
spending enough time chasing women without him, boosting
profits for the condom industries and making it quite obvious
they were men on the prowl the majority of the time. He
cringed at the reputations some of them had.

And he had been quick to assure them that his decision to
not bed women as often as they did had nothing to do with
Danielle McKay, the woman who had walked off, leaving
him standing at the altar ten years ago at a church filled with
over two hundred guests. The really sad thing was that his
family had liked her, until they'd discovered the truth as to
why she had walked out on him in front of everyone with an
"I'm sorry," instead of an "I do."

She had later confessed to having an affair that had resulted in a pregnancy. To her credit, at least she'd had the decency to not go through with the wedding instead of passing the kid off as his. But what his family hadn't known and what he'd kept hidden was that it had been a sense of obligation and not love that had driven him to ask Danielle to marry him in the first place. So in reality, her calling off the wedding had been a blessing in disguise.

He pulled in a deep breath. If anything, thoughts of Danielle should have reduced the size of his erection but they hadn't. That meant thoughts of Chloe outweighed thoughts of Danielle by a large margin. He doubted Danielle ever got him this aroused without even touching her. As far as he was concerned, this sort of physical reaction to a woman had to be cruel and unusual punishment.

Ramsey moved toward the bed, swearing with every step. He had to get up just as early as Chloe did. There were early morning chores that had to be done. Already a few of his nosy family members had called asking questions after a number of his men had bragged about his new cook and how pretty she was. News carried in Westmoreland Country and no doubt some were anticipating his next move and taking bets as to how quick he would be getting her from under his roof.

As far as he was concerned that was a no-brainer. She was definitely on her way out of there. He was determined that no matter what, he would be contacting the employment agency about finding him a replacement.

Four

When Chloe heard a sound behind her she didn't stop beating the huge bowl full of eggs because she knew who it was. She was determined that nothing about Ramsey Westmoreland was going to unnerve her today. After all, he wasn't the only man alive with a lot of sexual appeal, although he happened to be the only one who seemed to hold her interest.

She considered turning around to greet him and then decided because he was the one who'd entered the kitchen, he should be the one to make the gesture. If he didn't, it wouldn't be any sweat off her back, namely because she didn't have any sweat left after those naughty dreams last night where he'd had a starring role.

"Morning."

Okay, he'd done the proper thing and spoke first, but did he have to do so with such a deep huskiness in his voice? Such raw sexuality in his tone? It had only been one word for crying out loud. Yet the sound that had emitted from his lips was sending shudders through her body and had the potential to do other things she just didn't want to think about this early in the morning. It wasn't even four yet. And it was going to be a busy morning and an even busier noon.

Reluctantly, she turned around, deciding she would at least return his greeting. "Good—"

She swallowed the other word. And was that a moan she'd heard that had just passed her lips? Ramsey Westmoreland had the nerve, the sheer audacity to be standing in the middle of the kitchen putting on a shirt. At least now he was buttoning it up. But not before she'd caught a glimpse of his naked chest, ultra-fine biceps, sculpted shoulders and muscular arms. And it didn't help matters that his jeans were riding low on his hips and he was barefoot. It was quite obvious he had just taken a shower and had shaved. But still, he had that early-morning take-me-as-I-am look and she was tempted to do just that.

She wished she had the strength not to let her gaze hone in on such a powerful muscled body, but you could call her weak and she would answer. She was seeing firsthand why she wanted him as her *Simply Irresistible* man.

His gaze met hers when he'd noticed her looking and held on to her eyes until the last button was done. What a pity, she thought. She had enjoyed the show.

"I can't believe you beat me up," he said, now slipping a belt through the loops of his jeans.

Chloe wondered if it was the norm for him to get dressed in the middle of his kitchen. "I couldn't sleep," she decided to say. "Unfamiliar bed." There was no reason to tell him what had really kept her awake.

"But you did get enough sleep to function this morning," he stated. "The men will be hungry," he added.

She snorted, not caring how it sounded. "Mama Francine said men are always hungry. Even when their stomachs are full."

He leaned against the counter. "And who is Mama Francine?"

Too late she realized she might have said too much, but quickly decided telling him about Mama Francine wasn't giving anything away. "She's the person who taught me how to cook."

He nodded and she turned back to her eggs. She wasn't sure how many men would want their eggs scrambled, but she wanted to have the mixture ready just in case. And Mama Francine had taught her how to flip eggs, so those who didn't want their egg scrambled could tell her just how they liked it.

She heard him move, but refused to look up again. Besides, she knew he was moving toward her with a slow walk and glancing around inspecting everything while doing so. And with every step he took closer to her she felt his heat. It was even more powerful than what the stove was generating.

"I'm impressed."

She couldn't help but smile as she glanced over her shoulder. "Again?"

"Yep. You're serving both bacon and sausage."

She lifted a brow. Curious. "Something's wrong with that?"

He shrugged. "No. It's just that usually Nellie did one or the other."

She gazed him a pointed look. "Well, I'm not Nellie."

His heavy-lidded eyes raked over her. Slowly. Thoroughly. Then he said in a voice drenched with masculine awareness. "I can see that."

She didn't know what to say to that, so she said nothing at all before turning back around, placing the egg mixture aside to give attention to the pan of biscuits.

She knew he was staring at her legs and was tempted to pull her skirt down. However, doing so would give him the impression she was uncomfortable with what she was wearing. She wasn't nor should she be. It was a decent length and, therefore, it was appropriate. It hit just a little above the knee, but she was wearing leggings underneath. If he were to see her in some of the other outfits she owned, the ones that barely covered her thighs, he would probably be shocked.

"And we're getting homemade biscuits, too?"

She couldn't help the grin that touched her lips when she moved to open the oven door and slide the pan of biscuits inside. "Another abnormality?"

"Around here, yes."

That made Chloe wonder why this Nellie didn't prepare more of a variety of foods for breakfast. After closing the oven door she turned around, trying to ignore how responsive certain parts of her body were to Ramsey's nearness. He looked like he needed another five hours of sleep to do him justice, yet at the same time he looked sexy as sin. "May I ask you a question, Ramsey?"

He shrugged those massive shoulders again. "Depends on what you want to know."

She crossed her arms under her breasts and wondered if that had been a good thing when his eyes, half-asleep or not, followed the movement and seemed to be staring right through the material of her blouse to her nipples. At least the nipples thought so and were tingling at the attention they were getting. They were tingling and getting hard all at the same time.

"I want to know why this Nellie didn't offer more of a variety to the men at breakfast time."

She watched as a grin quirked his lips. "If you knew Nellie you wouldn't have to ask that question."

She rolled her eyes. "I don't know Nellie, so I'm asking it."

He tilted his head to the side, focusing those ever-so-intense eyes on her. And weakling that she was, immediately felt her body's response to his gaze. She wondered if he could detect it. It seemed so unreal that she would react to him this way when Daren couldn't get a spark of response out of her no matter how much he tried. But then, he hadn't tried too often. He'd been more interested in building his political future by parading Senator Burton's daughter out in front of those he felt he needed to impress. And when they were alone he was more into surfing the Internet for political blogs than getting into her. And those times when he had given her his attention, he might as well not have bothered. To say Daren hadn't had a romantic bone in his body was an understatement. However, the final straw came when he'd actually suggested they participate in a threesome. He claimed that kind of sexual kinkiness was a total turn on for him. For a man who couldn't even handle a twosome to fix his mouth to propose such a thing was too much. She'd sent him packing with the few items he had kept at her place and with a clear understanding not to come back.

Since then she had to focus all her energy—sexual and otherwise—into making her magazine a success and refused to think about having any type of a relationship with a man, and now, here she was, behaving like some supercharged, highly-sexed woman, ready to unzip his pants and jump his bones.

"Nellie figured that for breakfast she would give them just the basic, enough to get by so they could really be hungry by lunchtime," he interrupted her thoughts by stating.

She raised a brow. In her opinion that didn't make much sense. "Wouldn't they be hungry at lunchtime anyway?"

"Yes."

Chloe opened her mouth to say something, then snapped it shut, deciding to leave it alone. She and Nellie were two different people and the way the woman ran her kitchen was none of Chloe's business. Chloe's concern, her aim, was to make sure by the time she confessed who she was, Ramsey would feel he was irrevocably in her debt. And if offering the men who worked for him a variety at breakfast was going to get brownie points with him, then so be it. Besides, after listening to the men yesterday, it was quite obvious that most of them would like a home-cooked meal and she had no problem giving them one. Besides, being back in the kitchen had made her realize just how much she enjoyed cooking.

She heard the sound of a vehicle pulling up. "Sounds like your men are starting to arrive."

He shook his head. "No, it's Callum. He always arrives earlier than the others. He and I usually have business to discuss in the mornings."

She nodded. She had noticed the man yesterday and could tell he and Ramsey had more than just an employer-employee relationship. They seemed to be close friends. "He's from the Outback, isn't he?"

Ramsey had moved to where the coffeepot was sitting to pour a cup of coffee. He took a sip and frowned. The woman could even make damn good coffee. "Yes," he finally said, answering her question.

Few people, including some members of Ramsey's own

family, knew that Callum was a millionaire in his own right and owned a vast amount of land in Australia. He had several sheep ranches in Australia that were run by a very efficient staff. There was no need to tell her that the Aussie donated to charity the salary he earned as Ramsey's ranch manager.

Callum, at thirty-four, was the product of a wealthy white Australian father and an African American mother. His family had made billions in the sheep ranching business. Another thing she didn't need to know was that the only reason Callum was still hanging around here instead of moseying it back to Australia was because he didn't plan to leave without Gemma going with him.

Callum knew Ramsey well enough to know that when it came to his three sisters, Ramsey was a tad overprotective and would stop any advances on Megan, Gemma or Bailey cold. It had taken the Aussie a full year to convince Ramsey that his intentions toward Gemma were honorable and that he loved her and wanted to marry her. Both Ramsey and Dillon had given Callum their blessings for a marriage; however, they'd made it clear the final decision would be Gemma's. His sister had never given any indication that she was the least bit interested in Callum and was virtually clueless in regards to Callum's interest in her. As far as Ramsey was concerned maybe that was a good thing because Gemma was known to be a handful at times and would definitely have a lot to say about it; especially when she'd stated on more than one occasion that she never intended to ever give her heart to any man. That meant the Aussie had his work cut out for him if he intended to win her over.

Ramsey glanced around the kitchen before returning his gaze to Chloe. "It seems that you have everything under control."

"Sorry you thought that I wouldn't."

The mockery of her words had him frowning. Something told him that when it came to an attitude, hers was worse than his sister's. "It's not that I thought you wouldn't, Chloe. I think you more than proved your capabilities yesterday."

She lifted her chin. "Then what is it with you?"

He could pretend he had no idea what she was talking about, but he didn't. If the truth be told, he was the one with the attitude and was well aware it had probably been the pits since their initial meeting. He wasn't used to having to deal with a woman who made men pause when she walked into a room. A woman who wore her sexuality like it was a brand with her name on it. A woman who even now had blood surging through his veins.

And a woman he wanted to kiss.

His heart was racing at the very thought of locking his mouth with hers, and he knew at that moment if she stayed another night under his roof he would be doing that very thing if for no other reason than to get her out of his system. It would only be right to give her fair warning.

"How old are you, Chloe?"

From her expression he could tell she was wondering what her age had to do with anything. "I'm twenty-eight."

He nodded slowly, while his gazed continued to hold hers. "Then I would think you'd know what it is with me. But just in case you don't have a clue, I'll show you later."

Chloe felt a slow burn in her midsection followed by the feel of her heart thudding erratically in her chest. The meaning behind his words was pretty clear. If it hadn't been, then his eyes would have spelled things out for her. She could see the promises in the dark depths. Promises he wasn't trying to hide. Promises he intended to keep.

Before she could level a response the back door opened and Callum Austell walked in. He looked first at her and then at Ramsey. The smile that touched the man's lips would have been too deadly sexy if she hadn't thought Ramsey had a monopoly on sexiness.

"Ram. Chloe. Did I come at a bad time?" Callum asked in a low tone.

Chloe watched an irritated frown touch Ramsey's features and she drew in a deep breath. Lucia had warned her that he was a private person and she wasn't sure just how he felt about his friend picking up on the sexual tension flowing between them. It was tension so thick you could probably cut it with a knife and then spread it on bread. Deciding she needed to play off Callum's words, make the man think he was wrong in his assumption, she turned to Callum, opened her mouth to speak, but Ramsey beat her to it.

"No, you didn't come at a bad time. Come on, Cal, let's have that meeting." He then sat the coffee cup he'd been holding on the counter with a thud and headed out of the room. He stopped and glanced over his shoulder at Callum who had halted beside her.

"You sure look nice this morning, Chloe," Callum said in a husky tone with his deep Australian accent.

Chloe glanced up at the handsome man whom she figured was a year or two younger than Ramsey and couldn't help wondering what he was about. Had he just delivered a polite comment or a blatant flirtation?

"You're wasting my time, Cal. Are we meeting or what?" Ramsey called out in a sharp tone.

Callum looked across the room at Ramsey and smiled. "We're meeting."

And then he moved to follow Ramsey out of the room.

* * *

Ramsey clenched his jaw until he was in the office and then he all but slammed the door shut before facing Callum. The other man had the nerve, the very audacity, the damn gall, to smile. "What the hell was that about?" he asked through gritted teeth.

Callum gave him an innocent look, one Ramsey wasn't buying or selling. "I don't know what you mean, Ram."

Ramsey leaned back against his desk and frowned. "You were flirting with her."

Callum shrugged as another smile formed at the corners of his lips. "What if I was?"

Ramsey crossed his arms over his chest. "If you did it to get a rise out of me, then—"

"It worked," Callum taunted as he eased his muscular frame into a chair across from the desk. "Come on, Ram. Go ahead and admit you want the woman, which is why you're trying to get rid of her. When you know for yourself, even after eating just one meal, that she's a lot better cook than Nellie and her temperament is a vast improvement to what we're used to. I hate to say it but Nellie hasn't been missed around here and you know why."

Ramsey drew in a deep breath. Yes, he did know why. Nellie's disposition had begun deteriorating months ago after discovering her husband had been unfaithful to her. It was as if she had taken her hurt and anger out on the entire male population and his men knew it. They had tried being understanding, even sympathetic. But then after a while they'd become annoyed and just plain irritated. There was nothing worse than pissing a man off about his food.

Although Nellie's unexpected trip had placed him in a bind, he thought she needed the distance from his men for a while and vice versa. She still had a job when she returned, but the two of them would have a long talk first.

"Okay, so Nellie hasn't been missed, but when she comes back, she still has a job," he decided to speak up.

"Fine. Great. But in the meantime I think your men deserve a nice smile and friendly words every now and then, not to mention food they can eat without worrying about it being burned or overly seasoned."

Ramsey was silent.

"Look, I understand your problem with Chloe, Ram. Welcome to the club. I know how it is to want a woman so bad you ache," Callum said.

Ram frowned. He then narrowed his eyes on his friend. "You're referring to my sister," he said in a warning tone.

Callum snorted. "I'm referring to the woman I intend to marry who refuses to give me the time of day and it's getting damn near frustrating. Don't be surprised one day if you wake up and find us both gone." A smile touched Callum's lips. "I might resort to kidnapping."

Ram's frown deepened. "You'd better be joking." He then shook his head at Callum's outrageous threat. And then he couldn't help but chuckle. "Go ahead and kidnap her. I'll give you less than a week and you'll be bringing her back. Gemma will make your life a living hell if you did such a thing and I wouldn't be one to close my eyes on her if I were you. She likes getting even."

Ram smiled. Although he'd gone a little overboard he knew Callum got the picture. Of his three sisters, Gemma was the one who had a knack for not only speaking her mind but for backing up her thoughts. Callum knew this and was still in love with her. Go figure.

"Are you really thinking about letting Chloe go?" Callum

asked and Ramsey figured he was now desperate to change
the subject from Gemma back to Chloe. "I think it's a sin and
a shame that your men will have to suffer just because you
can't control your urges," Callum said.

Ramsey knew there was really no reason to deny what
Callum had just said. It was true. He was finding it hard to
control his urges around Chloe. And they were urges he'd
been controlling just fine before she'd shown up.

"The men are taking a bet as to how long we'll keep her."
Callum grinned and said, "I bet some will be surprised to
find her still here this morning."

Ramsey didn't see anything amusing. He didn't like being
reminded that others had noticed his interest in her yesterday.
"She's not the only good cook around these parts."

"I'm sure she isn't, but not many would want to have to
live on the ranch. Most would probably have homes of their
own; families they had to take care of when they left here
like Nellie." Callum rubbed his chin thoughtfully. "Um, that
makes me wonder."

Ramsey lifted a brow. "About what?"

"Why would a woman with her looks take a job where
she'll have to live here in the middle of nowhere for two solid
weeks. Doesn't she have any family?"

Ramsey considered Callum's question. To be honest Chloe's
personal life hadn't crossed his mind, mainly because he
hadn't intended for her to stay. In fact, he had planned to call
the employment agency when it opened this morning to see
how soon they could send a replacement. But Callum had
posed a good question. Evidently she did have a place in town
because she had returned last night with her luggage in tow.

"What if she's on the run and took the job to hide out
here?"

Ramsey looked over at Callum. "On the run from what?"

"An abusive husband. A psycho fiancé. A possessive boyfriend. Hell, I don't know, Ram. But if I were you I would find out."

Ramsey's frown hardened at the thought that Chloe might be running from a demented stalker. But then when he'd mentioned to her yesterday that she was hired as a live-in cook she'd seemed surprised. And last night she claimed that she'd only returned after deciding she didn't want to risk being late this morning. What if there was more than that?

"I don't think she's married or engaged because she's not wearing a ring and there's no indentation around her finger to indicate that she's worn one in the past," he said.

Callum chuckled. "You're as bad as Eric and Thel if you noticed all of that about a woman's finger."

Ramsey shrugged his shoulders, refusing to let Callum bait him. "Whatever."

"Well, it might be *whatever* if you don't find out. If you make her leave, then you could very well be sending her to her death."

Ramsey rolled his eyes. "Spare me the dramatics."

Callum stood. "Don't say I didn't warn you if something were to happen to her." He headed for the door.

Ramsey watched him about to leave. "Hey, where are you going? We haven't had our meeting yet."

Callum smiled over at him. "And we won't. At least not this morning. I smell homemade biscuits and *both* bacon and sausage. If you're still thinking about getting rid of her, then I need to make sure I eat well this morning. No telling what we might end up with for lunch."

Ramsey had always been a man who'd prided himself on two things: strength of mind and self-control. He felt both take a flying leap when he walked into the dining area an hour later. His men were gone and Chloe was clearing off the table. She glanced over in his direction and the moment he looked into her eyes, he wanted to cross the room and pull her to him and kiss her until she was nothing more than a limp body in his arms.

"You missed breakfast, but I kept you something warming in the oven. The eggs will be made to order," she said.

He nodded, surprised she had thought of him. "Thanks." He had deliberately remained in his office, trying to concentrate on finishing reports he had failed to do last night. His men's voices had carried to his office and he could tell from their conversations that they had enjoyed breakfast and were looking forward to lunch.

"Your men were wondering why you didn't eat breakfast with them."

He glanced over at her as he poured a cup of coffee, wondering if his men had been the ones speculating or if it had been her. "Were they?"

"Yes."

When he didn't say anything but sipped his coffee while watching her, she said. "If you're ready to eat I'll get your plate out of the oven."

"Thanks. I'd appreciate it."

He moved toward the table and after sitting down he watched her and wondered if Callum's speculations were true. Was she living here at the ranch as his cook because she was on the run from someone? He sipped his coffee thinking that he was not one to overreact, but what if some of what Callum assumed was true?

"How do you want your eggs, Ramsey?"

He blinked, realizing she had asked him a question. "Excuse me? What did you say?"

"Your eggs. Do you prefer scrambled, sunny-side up or over easy?"

It was on the tip of his tongue to say he preferred them *over her* so he could lick them off, but thought better of it. She was wearing another short dress and like last night she had spoiled the effect by a pair of leggings. What was with those things? Why the hell were women wearing them under their dresses? He enjoyed seeing bare skin. Nothing was wrong with seeing a nice piece of feminine flesh on occasion. And although he'd never seen her legs, he had no reason to believe they weren't gorgeous, a real arousal-getter just like the rest of her.

The lower part of his body was already throbbing with the way her outfit fit over her bottom, showing a perfect shape. He could just imagine lying in bed with that backside curved against his front in spoon fashion, dipping his head to nibble on her neck and to place marks of passion there before moving toward...

"Ramsey?"

He blinked again. "Yes?"

"How do you want your eggs?"

"Sunny-side up will be fine."

He watched how she handled the frying pan. There was no doubt in his mind she knew what she was doing. And the way she cracked the egg was sure and precise. He couldn't help wondering about her cooking skills. Had she gone to culinary school? If so, why wasn't she working at a first-class restaurant somewhere? Why was she here on a sheep ranch on the outskirts of Denver? There was only one way to find out. He'd discovered that with some women if you got them talking they would tell you just about anything you wanted to know. It worked with Bailey, although it hadn't been a proven trick with Megan or Gemma.

As she cooked his eggs he studied her. She didn't look like a woman under any sort of duress. She seemed calm and looked cool. And she appeared to enjoy what she was doing.

His gaze moved to her face. She didn't have normal features. She was beautiful. Soft-looking brown skin, a sensual pair of eyes, a cute nose and a pair of lips he longed to taste. Her dark brown hair was shoulder length, lustrous curly strands. It didn't take much to imagine that hair spread across a pillow. His pillow. And those sensual dark eyes shimmering with arousal right as she shifted her body to spread her thighs, open her legs to fill the air with her scent while he stared down at her feminine mound, moist, ready, waiting for him to sample.

The surge of desire that swept through him at that moment was so fierce it almost took his breath away. He needed something stronger than a cup of coffee and was tempted to pull a beer out of the refrigerator. Instead he drew in a long, deep breath, shifted his gaze to look out the window. Think about something else. The bill that was soon to come due on his new tractor. The fact that Gemma was bugging him about decorating the rest of his house. Anything except making hot, carnal love to Chloe.

Trying to regain control of his libido and senses, he looked over toward her. She might know how to wield a frying pan and all that, but there was a refined air about her that disconnected her ability in the kitchen with the way she carried herself. It was as if she should be getting served instead of being the one doing the serving. "Are you married?"

She glanced over at him but only for a second. She went back to concentrating on cooking his eggs. "No."

"You sure?"

Her head lifted and she stared at him, gave him a look like he'd suddenly grown two heads or something. "Of course I'm sure." She held up her left hand. "See, no ring."

He shrugged. "That doesn't mean anything these days."

She frowned as she slid his egg from the frying pan onto the plate. "It would mean something to me."

"Okay, so you're not married. Are you involved in a serious relationship?"

She set the plate in front of him and gave him a pointed look. "Is there a reason for these questions?"

He smiled. Because she asked he might as well go ahead and tell her. She was mature enough to handle it. "Yes, there's a reason. When I get around to kissing you I'll feel better knowing your mouth doesn't belong to any other man. Legally or otherwise."

She didn't say anything for a moment. Then she opened her mouth, probably to tell him just where he could take his own mouth—legally or otherwise—but instead of saying anything right then, she just tightened her lips together.

He chuckled. "Tightening those lips shut won't keep me from prying them apart for a kiss if that's what I want to do, Chloe."

Chloe folded her arms across her chest. "Is there a reason for this madness?"

"Is that what this is? Madness?" he asked as he began eating.

She lifted her chin and glared at him. "You got another name for it?"

"What about hunger?"

She frowned. "Hunger?"

"Yes, hunger of a sexual nature. I need to get you out my

system and I figured I'll start by kissing you to see if that will work."

Chloe dropped her hands by her side. Not believing he'd said such a thing. And not believing her heart was thumping rapidly in her chest at the thought of him making good on his threat. "You're nothing like Daren."

He raised a dark brow. "Who's Daren?"

"The last guy I was involved with."

Ramsey ignored the twinge of jealousy that invaded his gut. "Is not being like Daren good or bad?"

She shrugged. "Not sure. Although, I think it would have been nice if he would have had even a fraction of that *hunger* thing."

He immediately caught on to what she'd insinuated. "I can't imagine any man hanging around you for long without wanting to gobble you alive. He must have been a real idiot."

Chloe kept herself from smiling and refused to admit she'd thought the same thing. "He had his own ideas about what down to earth lovemaking was about. He suggested that we participate in a threesome."

Ramsey frowned. He could handle the fact that her ex-boyfriend hadn't had a passionate bone in his body, but the thought that the man had actually wanted to share her with someone else was as demented as it could get. No man in his right mind would share her.

"Then he wasn't just an idiot," Ramsey spoke up to say. "He was a crazy idiot. Any man who could get it into his mind to share you evidently doesn't have the brain he was born with. There's no way I would consider doing such a thing. I would want you all to myself."

His gaze roamed over her. "It would be me and me alone who would leave a satisfied smile on your lips, Chloe."

Chloe felt a tightening in her stomach as his gaze slowly swept over her, lingering in certain places and bestowing a visual caress in others. And his deep seductive voice was stirring all kinds of sensations to life inside her.

"How long were you with this guy?"

She wondered why he wanted to know. "A year."

"And how long have the two of you been apart?"

Chloe wasn't sure why he wanted to know that, either. Why she'd even shared anything with him about Daren in the first place was a mystery to her. But she had and evidently he was curious. "Two years. Now if you will excuse me I'm about to tackle the dishes."

Ramsey watched her walk off over to the sink and, since she was doing her best to ignore him, he dug into his meal. Not surprisingly, everything was delicious and for the first time in a long while, he was enjoying his food. He was also enjoying watching Chloe while he ate. If she only knew all the things that were running through his mind while chewing on a piece of bacon and swallowing his toast.

She refused to look over at him which was probably a good thing. Instead she was trying to keep busy and continued to ignore him in the process. By the time he had finished breakfast and drained the last of his coffee, she had stacked all the dishes on the counter to load into the huge dishwasher. She wiped down the countertops until they gleamed.

Getting up from the table he crossed the kitchen to the sink to place his plate and cup in the sudsy water. And when he turned toward her she made a quick move to get out of his way. She wasn't fast enough and he reached out and took hold of her hand.

A shiver immediately rushed down Chloe's spine and she sucked in a sharp breath the instant Ramsey touched her.

She tilted her head and looked up at him. He was standing in front of her and his gaze, she noticed, was intense as ever and centered directly on her lips. Then his eyes moved slowly up her face to her eyes. He smiled and then slid his gaze back down to her lips again.

She knew at that moment he was about to make good on his threat to kiss her. Heat began formulating at the center of her thighs, and the way he was staring at her lips made her hot. Wet. Then something within her began to ache. It was a hollowed emptiness she just realized was there. He moved a step closer and his scent inflamed everything within her, pulling her into the depths of his masculinity, swirling her about and drawing her under into his sensual spell.

She studied him, became enmeshed in the starkly strong features of his face. He was a very handsome man, so much so that her senses were betraying her, refusing to let her do the right thing and demand he remove his hand from hers. Instead she felt herself easing toward him at the same time he shifted his body even closer to hers.

Chloe found herself pinned between him and the counter, felt the hardness of his erection come to rest between her thighs like it had every right to be there. For the first time in her life she felt totally in sync with a man, fully aware of who he was and what he could do. And the thought of what he could do, what he *would* do sent an intense shiver up her spine. It made her anxious to the point where she felt her nerves beginning to quiver. She swallowed deeply and when that didn't help her she took her tongue and swiped it across her lower lip.

Not a good move.

She looked into his face and saw the effect doing such a thing had on him. By no means was she trying to encourage him and when she saw heat flare in his eyes, she knew something elementally male was taking place and he had no intention of fighting it.

He leaned forward and before she could catch her next breath, he bent his head and captured her lips.

Five

Ramsey had told Chloe this wasn't madness, but at that moment he knew that quite possibly it was worse. There was no way to explain why the moment his lips touched hers he'd felt something he couldn't name or define slid up his spine. And her taste—rich, honeyed and sweet—drove him to stroke his tongue all over her mouth, sample her everywhere, taste her, and with a greed that made him groan. And when he released his hold on her wrist to place his hands at the center of her back, he shifted positions as fire spread through him.

Energy he didn't think he had, especially after a sleepless night, raced through him, gripped him hard, made his erection swell that much more. He wanted to think this was ludicrous, but he knew this was as sexual as it could get, as he took her mouth in a hot and urgent kind of way. He was determined to make her feel all the things he was feeling at that moment. And when she took hold of his tongue, he knew he'd succeeded.

The hands at her back became possessive, they lowered to cup her backside and she moaned at the same time she moved against him. They were chest to breast, hip to thigh, with mouths locked tight and tongues mingling wildly. He'd said he was sexually hungry and he was proving just how famished he was.

And the way his hands were now moving over her, as if outlining the shape of her bottom, was driving him insane. He was becoming acquainted with her curves and all her soft yielding flesh. There was no doubt in his mind that while he took her mouth with a passion, she could feel his aroused body part pressing deeply into the juncture of her legs as if that was where it belonged.

He heard the moans coming from her throat and every time one escaped he deepened the kiss that much more. He was tempted to spread her out on the kitchen table at that very moment and have his way with her. Take her with a passion until he was too weak to stand.

"We could always leave and come back later."

The heavy voice made them jump apart like kids who'd gotten caught with their hands in the cookie jar. Filled with both anger and protectiveness Ramsey moved in front of Chloe while glaring at his brothers, Zane and Derringer, and his cousin Jason.

"What the hell are the three of you doing here?"

Derringer smiled. "We had a meeting. You told us to be here at seven. Sharp. Threatened us with dire straits if we were late. Did you forget?"

He had.

"We can understand if you did forget," Zane said. He was two years younger than Ramsey and known as a smart-mouth.

"It's no big deal, Ram," Jason said. Jason was the easy-going cousin and his trademark smile was genuine. "It would be nice if you introduced us," Jason added.

"Yeah," Zane said grinning. "Any reason you're hiding her behind your back?"

Cursing quietly, Ramsey realized he was doing that very thing. He stepped aside and the moment his brothers' eyes lit on Chloe, all three gave her an appreciative male perusal. He loved every member of his family, but at that moment thoughts of doing these three in actually made him want to smile.

"Chloe, I want you to meet my brothers, Zane and Derringer, and my cousin Jason." And then to his brothers and cousin, he said. "Guys, this is Chloe Burton, my new cook."

Chloe had never been so embarrassed in her entire life and actually felt the color stain her already-dark skin. From the way the three were staring at her she could only assume that they'd never walked in on Ramsey kissing a woman before.

She extended her hand to them. "How do you do?"

Their handshakes were firm and as she locked eyes with each of them she saw a friendliness in their dark depths. And there was no doubt in her mind that when placed in the same room with a crowd anyone could easily guess they were related. They all had the same chiseled jaw, dark brown eyes, dimpled smile and creamy brown skin. They were extremely handsome men. Her gaze was momentarily drawn back to Derringer, the man who had her best friend's heart and he didn't even know it.

"Okay, so much for introductions," Ramsey broke into her thoughts and said aloud. "Let's have that meeting."

Zane, she noticed, was still holding on to her hand. He smiled, glanced over at Ramsey and said, "The three of you can have a meeting. I prefer staying here with Chloe. I hear she can whip up the best scrambled eggs this side of the Rockies."

She watched Ramsey tip his head back and sigh. He then fixed his brother a leveled stare. "Don't push things with me, Zane."

Zane drew his gaze from Ramsey and glanced down at Chloe. She thought the smile that tugged at his lips was devilish. "What about a rain check, Chloe? Tomorrow perhaps?"

She could only nod and then watched the three men follow Ramsey from the room.

"That pretty much sums things up," Jason was saying. "I talked to Durango and McKinnon yesterday and they are excited at the prospect of expanding their operation to Colorado."

Ramsey nodded. Durango Westmoreland and McKinnon Quinn were cousins of theirs, Durango by blood and McKinnon by marriage. The two lived in Montana and owned M&D, a very successful horse breeding and training operation. A few years ago they had invited another cousin, Clint Westmoreland, who lived in Texas, to join their million-dollar business. And now they were making the same offer to Zane, Derringer and Jason. The three had traveled to Bozeman and spent three weeks with Durango and McKinnon and their families, learning more about the operation and to determine if it was a business venture they wanted to become a part of. As all three were fine horsemen, Ramsey couldn't imagine their turning down the offer.

"So the three of you are really thinking about doing it?" he asked as he looked over the report. Everything was in order and M&D was doing extremely well; especially after Prince

Charming, a horse they had trained for Sheikh Jamal Yasir—another cousin by marriage—had placed in the Kentucky Derby.

"Yes, and we figured since our three properties are adjacent to each other," Jason was saying, "we can share acreage for grazing land and for future expansions. But what we don't want to do is to reduce the land you need for your sheep."

Ramsey nodded, appreciating their concern. Sheep required a lot of land and his siblings and cousins had been very generous in letting him use some of theirs for grazing purposes. At present he was satisfied with the number of sheep he owned, and other than the lambs due to be born at the end of the month, he didn't intend to increase his herd anytime soon.

"With what Dillon and I own together, there will be plenty enough," he said to the three. "And before Bane took off for the Navy he gave Dillon permission for me to use his land if there was a need. A few days ago I received a letter notifying me that the federal government has approved my use of land at Diamond Ridge, so I'll start taking part of the herd there later this year for grazing."

Ramsey glanced back down at the report. "Although I have my hands full here with the sheep, I'll be interested in becoming a silent partner with the M&D Colorado-based operation once it gets started. I think it's time that I consider diversifying. It's not good to have all your eggs in one basket."

"True," Zane nodded, casting his brother a smile. "We would love to have you on board. And speaking of eggs, you kind of got uptight when I invited myself to breakfast."

Ramsey snorted as he leaned back in his chair. "What is

it with you and Callum with your crazy games? Chloe is off limits."

Derringer, who was slouched down on the love seat, glanced over at Ramsey and asked in a belligerent tone. "Says who?"

Ramsey frowned. Derringer was younger than him by three years and enjoyed being argumentative. "Says me, Derringer. Evidently you either didn't get it or you didn't understand the message I gave Zane in the kitchen."

"So, you're saying Chloe is more than just your cook?" Jason asked, as if for clarification.

Ramsey hauled in a deep breath, irritated at the thought of having to explain anything to his relatives. But knowing them the way he did, he knew he'd better do so. There was no doubt in his mind that there would be more explaining to do to the others when word got around that these three had walked in on him kissing Chloe. Zane was probably just itching to tell everyone, especially because it had been eons since Ramsey had been involved with a woman.

"Chloe is nothing more than my cook," he said.

Now it was Zane who snorted. "I don't recall you ever kissing Nellie."

Ramsey rolled his eyes. "Nellie is a married woman."

Derringer straightened in his seat and lifted a brow. "Are you saying if she wasn't married you'd be kissing her?"

Before he could respond Zane burst out laughing while slapping his thigh. "Damn, Ramsey, we didn't know you had it in you. And all this time we figured you were living a dull and sexually inactive life."

Ramsey took a deep, calming breath. His brothers were trying to get a rise out of him and he refused to fall prey to their tactics any more than he had to Callum's earlier. He tossed the document he was holding on his desk. "Let me get something straight. The kiss the three of you walked in on was something that just happened. Chloe is my cook and nothing more. She'll be living here for two weeks until Nellie returns."

He then leaned forward to make sure they heard his next words clearly. "However, since I know how two of the three of you operate, I want to make it clear here and now that she is *not* open game. You're all welcome to breakfast, lunch or dinner at any time, as always. But that's all you're welcome to."

"Um, that sounds kind of territorial, Ram," Zane said, eyeing his brother.

Ramsey shrugged. "Think whatever you like, just make sure you heed my warning."

Later that evening Chloe went into Ramsey's living room and sat on the sofa with a glass of wine in her hand. She curled her feet beneath her as she took a sip. It felt good to relax after a tiring day.

Although she enjoyed being in the kitchen, spending her time cooking for a group of men was not how she had envisioned her month-long vacation. Especially one that had started off in the Bahamas.

But she would have to admit that just seeing the satisfied grins on Ramsey's men's faces when they had eaten breakfast that morning and lunch at noon had been worth all the time she had spent over a stove.

The men asked her to make more homemade biscuits in the morning, and they liked having a choice of bacon and sausage. She would surprise them tomorrow by going a step further and making omelets.

She had checked with her office in Florida and had spoken

briefly to her editor-in-chief. Everything was going fine, which Chloe wasn't surprised about. She had an efficient team who ran things whether she was in the office, and that's the way she wanted it. Her father had told her time and time again that to be successful as CEO of your own company, you needed a good team working for you who could handle just about anything in your absence. She had built *Simply Irresistible* to the magazine it was and was using her time expanding the market area.

Her thoughts shifted from the magazine to Ramsey and the kiss they had shared earlier that day. It was the kiss that three members of his family had witnessed. She could just imagine how Ramsey felt about it, which was probably the reason he had avoided her most of the day. He hadn't dined with his men at lunch and he hadn't returned to the ranch since she had noticed his leaving early that afternoon.

She couldn't help wondering if the kiss had worked and she was out of his system. She might be out of his, but now he was deeply embedded into hers. Never had she been kissed so thoroughly before. Never had a man explored her mouth the way he had, in such a blatantly carnal way. There had not been anything traditional about his kiss. He had delivered it with an expertise that had left her panting for hours. She had been both affected and infected by his kiss. Even now her lips were still tingling.

She would be the first to admit things were not going as she planned with him. She had been attracted to him from the first, so there was no surprise at that. But what had been a surprise, totally unexpected, was the degree of hot tension that surrounded them whenever they were in the same room. Or her to be thinking about jumping his bones whenever she saw him. In her line of business, she met plenty of good-looking men. But none had ever sparked her interest, or stimulated a deep attraction the way Ramsey had.

How was she supposed to live under his roof, breathe the same air, when sexual thoughts constantly flowed through her mind? And unfortunately that kiss had been the icing on the cake. There was no doubt in her mind that she was now addicted to his taste as well as to his masculine scent.

Chloe's thoughts shifted back to what Ramsey had said about never sharing her with anyone. There had been something about it that had touched her. She drew in a deep breath at the realization that something about Ramsey was getting to her. And she knew at that moment that he was a man in a way that Daren could never be. Ramsey was someone who could and would take care of his own. That was evident by the way he had taken on the responsibility of raising his siblings. Although he could be brusque at times, she believed he didn't have a selfish bone in his body.

And knowing that was what was endearing him to her.

She felt panic in her chest at the thought that anything about Ramsey was endearing to her, but as much as she wanted to deny it she knew it was true. There were so many things about him that reminded him of her father—especially his sense of what was right. She'd seen it in the way he treated his men and his family.

She took another sip of wine. Later she would call Lucia to let her know she'd met Derringer and thought he was definitely a cutie. Although Ramsey had given his brothers and cousin a hard time, she could easily pick up on the love and mutual respect between the four men. And all four were extremely handsome.

But still in her book, Ramsey was her choice. There was something about him that made her heart pound in her chest each and every time she saw him. Maybe the best thing would be to abandon the idea of his posing for the cover of her magazine. She should go ahead and tell him the truth tonight and be packed and ready to leave. But if she did that, it would leave him in a bind. His men were counting on her to provide them with a delicious breakfast in the morning and a tasty meal at lunch. Besides, she was not a quitter, so no matter how tough things got she would not throw in the towel.

She leaned over and placed her glass of wine on the coffee table when she heard her cell phone go off. She pulled it out of her skirt pocket and smiled when she saw the call was from her father.

"Dad, how are you?"

"I'm doing fine. Just where the heck are you, Chloe Lynn?"

She chuckled. Nobody but her father called her by her first and middle names. Only after she'd finished college and started her business did she appreciate what an outstanding man and wonderful person her father was. He had entered politics when she had been in her last year of high school and now he was in his third term as Senator and swore it was the last, but she knew better.

He had always encouraged her to do whatever it was in life that she wanted to do and not live under his shadow as the "senator's daughter." She had gone to the college she had wanted to attend and had gotten the degree in just what she'd wanted. The only thing he flexed his muscles about was his belief in helping others during her summers. In the end she'd never regretted doing so.

"I'm in Denver for now."

"And when will you be coming home?"

She raised a brow. Home for her had always been Tampa,

but for her father since becoming Senator Jamison Burton, he'd stayed in D.C. most of the time. "Not sure when I'll be back in Tampa. Why? What's going on?"

He paused and then said, "I intend to ask Stephanie to marry me tonight, and was hoping you would be here in case she said yes, so we can all celebrate."

Chloe's smile widened. Her father had been dating Circuit Court of Appeals judge Stephanie Wilcox. A fifty-something divorced mother of a son and a daughter in their twenties, her father and Stephanie had been dating for a few years and Chloe had wondered when he would consider asking the woman to share his life.

"That's wonderful, Dad. Congratulations. I'm sorry I won't be there to celebrate, but please make sure you let Stephanie know how happy I am for both of you."

Ten minutes later she was still smiling when she slipped her phone back into her skirt pocket. Finally, her father was about to commit his life to something other than politics and she was happy about it. He had remained a widower and she had often wondered why, when he would be such a good catch for someone. But she'd heard over the years from both sets of grandparents how much he'd loved her mother and he hadn't wanted to give his heart to another woman. It had taken Stephanie three years, but she had done what some would have thought as impossible.

"After all the work that went into feeding my men breakfast and lunch you have a reason to smile?"

Startled, Chloe inclined her head to glance across the room. She hadn't heard the door open and now Ramsey was standing in the doorway and looking at her.

Refusing to be rattled, she reached for her glass of wine and took a sip, not sure how she would answer his question. There was no way she could share her father's good news on the risk that he might ask questions she didn't want to answer. All he would have to do is to go on the Internet and do a search on her father to discover she was his daughter and exactly what she did for a living.

"That's not what the smile is for," she decided to say. "I just received a call from a friend to say he was asking his girl to marry him tonight. And I'm happy for both of them."

She watched as he crossed the room to sit in the chair across from the sofa. She tried not to stare and was surprised he was giving her the time of day when it was obvious he'd been avoiding her earlier, especially after their kiss.

"I guess getting married would make some folks happy," he said.

She took another sip of her wine while holding his gaze, trying not to dwell on just how good he looked while he leaned back in the chair with muscled shoulders, hard jeans-clad thighs and long legs stretched to where his booted feet touched a portion of the coffee table. She wondered if he realized he was still wearing his Stetson. "Um. But I take it that you're not one of them," she replied.

"Nope, I wouldn't be one of them. I intend to be a single man for the rest of my days."

She considered his words. "So, you're one of those men who have a problem with matrimony? Who thinks marriage isn't a big deal?"

He lifted a brow. "And you're one of those women who thinks that it is?"

"I asked you first."

Yes, she had, Ramsey thought. His first inclination was to ignore the question. Move on to something else. And a part of him wondered what the hell he was doing here, sitting across from her at all. Especially because he'd taken great pains to make sure their paths didn't cross after his brothers and cousin had left. He hadn't liked the way Zane, Derringer and Jason's thoughts had been going. He would like to think he had put their false assumptions to rest, but he knew them well enough to know that was too much to hope for.

"Take your time if you need to gather your thoughts," Chloe said.

Ramsey kept his gaze trained on her. Unwavering. He couldn't give her a forced smile even if he'd wanted to because staying single was a serious topic with him. And it wasn't that he had a problem with matrimony per se, after the last fiasco of a wedding, he figured there was not a woman alive who would be able to get him back in a church for the sole purpose of getting hitched. No, he liked his single life just fine. He would think after dealing with the likes of an ex-boyfriend like Daren, so would she.

He continued to look at her, recalled her statement about gathering his thoughts and figured she would get along with his sisters easily because she seemed to have a smart mouth like them. That thought made his gaze shift to her lips.

He then swallowed, wishing he hadn't gone there with her mouth, especially because he knew how it tasted. And then there had been her response to him. He could do bodily harm to his kinfolk for their untimely interruption.

"I don't need to gather my thoughts," he finally said. Otherwise he would be tempted to cross the room and taste her again. "Raphael Westmoreland married enough for all of us."

She lifted a brow. "Raphael Westmoreland?"

"Yes, my great-grandfather. Rather recently we discovered he had a slew of wives. We also discovered he had a twin."

Evidently that sparked her interest, and her movement on the sofa sparked his. She slid closer to the edge and when she leaned forward her blouse gaped open a little, but enough to see some cleavage, as well as the thin pink fabric of her bra. Her skin looked velvety smooth, soft and a beautiful brown. He could imagine removing her bra and then lavishing her breasts with hot kisses, then taking his tongue and—

"Well?"

He blinked, reluctantly shifted his gaze from her chest to her eyes. They were bright. Inquiring. Intrigued. Apparently stuff about long-lost relatives interested her like it did the others in his family. Once they had become acquainted with the Atlanta Westmorelands, who were descendants of his great-grandfather's twin brother Reginald, Dillon had been eager to find out all that he could. His search to uncover the truth had led him to his wife Pamela. So in a way something good had come of it.

"Well, what?" he asked, deciding to play along just for the hell of it. Irritate her a bit. He liked the way her lips curved in a frown when she was aggravated about something. In addition to that, he liked her sexy pose on the sofa and the eager look on her face to find out more. Now if he could only get her out of wearing those damn leggings.

The glare she gave him denoted she was getting impatient, downright annoyed, at the length of time it was taking for him to tell her what she wanted to know. "Tell me some more about your great-grandfather's twin," she said with barely restrained impatience.

He could and would do so if it meant keeping her mind occupied while he continued to check her out. "We discovered over a year ago that our great-grandfather Raphael had a twin by the name of Reginald."

"And none of you had any idea?"

"No. Great-Grampa Raphael led everyone to believe he'd been born the only child. One of the Atlanta Westmorelands' genealogy search provided proof that Raphael and Reginald were twins and that Raphael had been considered the black sheep of the family after running off with a married woman. He finally settled here in Denver five wives later."

Ramsey paused when he felt a rush of sensations hammer his veins when Chloe shifted her body on the sofa once again and his gaze moved to her feet. They were bare and her toes were painted a prissy pink. When had seeing painted toes on a woman become so erotic?

He found it an effort to move his gaze from her feet back to her face, especially when his eyes had to pass over her chest. Of course it lingered awhile before moving on. When he finally settled on her eyes he saw hers were narrowed. "I'm sure there is more to this story," she said.

He nodded. "Of course and maybe one day I'll tell you the rest."

He had no idea why he'd said that. There wouldn't be a "one day" where they were concerned. Although he had changed his mind about calling the agency for another cook, he needed to keep his guard up around her. Yet here he was, misleading her into thinking he would share anything else about his family with her.

He eased out of his chair, deciding he'd said enough and had stayed in here with her longer than he'd needed to. Definitely longer than he should have. It then occurred to him he was still wearing his hat. Damn.

He took it off his head thinking the woman had a way of making him not think straight and that wasn't a good thing. "I'm taking a shower and going out to grab something for dinner," he said, and then wondered why on earth was he telling her his plans. His comings and goings were really none of her business.

He moved to leave the room and head upstairs, but her words stopped him. "I prepared dinner for you, Ramsey."

He stopped, turned and looked over at her. She was only getting paid to fix breakfast and lunch because his men usually ate dinner at their own homes with their families. Usually he dined at Penney's Diner a few miles down the road or with one of his family members.

"You didn't have to do that, Chloe."

"I know, but I wanted to because I need to eat, too," she replied, as if that explained things.

"Suit yourself," he said, knowing he sounded totally nonchalant and ungrateful when he was anything but. After spending practically her entire day in the kitchen preparing breakfast and lunch for his men, she had gone out of her way to prepare him dinner when she really didn't have to do it.

He turned in the direction of the kitchen and when he got to the edge of the room, he paused and then turned back around. She was staring into space as if she was trying to figure out in her own mind what had happened next with Raphael Westmoreland. She had moved from her earlier pose and was now curled up in the corner of his sofa, and every so often after taking a sip of wine her tongue would dart out to lick her top lip as if savoring the taste. Ramsey felt his body tighten with desire as he watched her.

"Chloe?"

She looked over at him and he could tell from her expression she was surprised to see him still standing there. "Yes?"

"Thanks for dinner." He then turned and kept walking toward the kitchen.

Hours later with his jaw clamped together tight, Ramsey walked the floor in his bedroom. This would be another night where he would not be getting any sleep and there was no excuse for it, and he needed his rest. The next two weeks of shearing would be both mind- and body-consuming if today was an example of what was to come.

At least his men had been excited about breakfast and lunch and had kept a steady conversation about both most of the day. Chloe's choice of food was a big hit and at quitting time today the men had been speculating on what they would be getting tomorrow for breakfast. Chloe was a definite asset to his ranch.

Ramsey moved over to the window to look out, not liking what he was thinking. She had done it again, he thought in disgust. The dinner she'd prepared for him had been the best he'd ever eaten, so much in fact that he'd been tempted to lick the plate. He had sat in the kitchen alone, not bothering to eat at the table, but had taken a stool at the breakfast bar instead.

Consuming his meal in silence he had been well aware of the moment she had come into the kitchen to wash out her wine glass. Mumbling a good-night, she had quickly left to head up the stairs. He had watched her go. Neither of them had mentioned anything about the kiss they'd shared earlier that day, and that was fine with him because his brothers and cousin had said enough. Not surprisingly, word of the kiss had reached Dillon and Callum. At least none of his sisters knew about it. Had they been privy to such information, they would have called by now, or even worse, just showed up to introduce themselves.

Hold up. Time out. He wasn't ready for something like that to happen, especially if his sisters assumed the wrong thing like Zane, Derringer and Jason had. But knowing Megan, Gemma and Bailey like he did, there was no doubt in his mind that they would have taken things further by trying to intentionally stir interest even if there wasn't any there.

At least he could safely say from his conversation with Chloe earlier that she was not a woman on the run as Callum had speculated. Other than what she'd told him about her ex-boyfriend, he still hadn't gotten her to talk a lot about herself, although she was trying to get all in his business about good old Raphael.

He shook his head. Other than knowing she was a damn good cook, she'd had an idiot of an ex-boyfriend, and that she had a friend who was getting married, he didn't know a lot about her. But then maybe the less he knew the better. She was doing a good job at what she had been hired to do.

Although he was losing sleep in the process.

But then, his inability to sleep and walking the floors at night was not her problem. He had to be the one who garnered more control. He had to stop the flow of sexual tension between them. But how? Imagining her with a sack over her head whenever he saw her wouldn't work because he would still be able to see her body. And there was no way he could look at all those curves without a degree of lust filling his head.

Sighing deeply, he made his way back to the bed. It was close to one in the morning and if he had to lie in bed, stare at the ceiling and count sheep to get to sleep, then so be it. Hell, sheep were his life anyway.

Chloe sat up in bed and clicked on her cell phone to answer it. She smiled when she saw the call was from her dad. "Okay, Pop, it's close to one in the morning here, which means it's later than that on the east coast, so this better be good."

Senator Burton's hearty laugh came in through the phone. "It is. I have Stephanie here with me. I asked her to marry me and she accepted and we just wanted our kids to know."

Tears she couldn't hold back came into Chloe's eyes. Her father sounded happy and if anyone deserved happiness it was him. She swiped at her tears and said, "I'm happy for you and Stephanie, Dad. Congratulations. Have the two of you told Brian and Danita yet?"

Brian and Danita were Stephanie's son and daughter. Brian was twenty-six and in his last year of medical school at the University of Florida. Danita was twenty-one and attending Xavier University of Louisiana. She, Brian and Danita got along marvelously and had been more than ready for their parents to take things to the next level. There was no doubt in Chloe's mind they would be as happy for their mother as she was for her dad.

"Not yet," her father said, interrupting her thoughts. "We thought we would call our oldest child first."

She smiled. Already he was thinking of them in terms of a family. "Okay, and I hate that I'm not there to celebrate, but when I return to Florida we're going to all get together."

"And when will you be returning to Florida?"

Chloe nibbled her bottom lip. That was a good question. "Not for at least another two weeks," she said with certainty. Ramsey's regular cook should have returned by then, and hopefully she would have come clean and told him the truth. She was hoping that once she made it clear he owed her, that he would do the cover and the article, grudgingly or otherwise.

"Okay, sweetheart. Stephanie wants to talk to you."

It was at least twenty minutes later before Chloe ended the call with the woman who would become her stepmother. They talked about plans for the wedding but only briefly because Danita's input would be needed on any major decisions.

She cuddled in bed wishing her own personal life could be as happy and exciting as her dad's. She took a long breath wondering where that yearning had come from. Probably with her dad's calling and then recalling her earlier conversation this evening with Ramsey about matrimony had stirred something within her, and it was something she hadn't thought about in a long time. It was her own desire to one day settle down, marry and have children. When things had ended with her and Daren, she hadn't given up on that dream. And although such a thing was not in her immediate plans, she still had that desire tucked away somewhere. What woman didn't? Even with her determination to be successful with her magazine company, she believed once that was achieved, she would find her Mr. Right. And one thing was for certain he definitely wouldn't be some surly sheep rancher.

But then if that was the case…and she was most certain that it was, why did she go to bed thinking about him every night? And why was the last thing she saw before closing her eyes his intense, penetrating dark eyes staring at her like they could see right through to her soul.

She closed her eyes. *Like now.* There he was, in vivid color, as he had been that evening, sitting across from her on the sofa with his legs stretched out in front of him, with his Stetson still on his head and looking sexier than any man had a right to look. So much in fact that more than once she had been tempted to get up off the sofa and go to him and curl up in his lap and purr.

She slowly opened her eyes, grateful she hadn't done such a thing. She really should thank him for keeping her agitated during most of the conversation, which stopped her from making a complete fool of herself. But if the truth be told, telling her about his great-grandfather had helped to refocus her attention. She knew there was more to the story and wondered why this was her first time hearing it. If such a thing hadn't come up on one of her computer's search engines that meant it hadn't made the news. Hmm. It was definitely something she would like to share with her readers, which might prompt them to want to start looking into their own family tree.

She shifted in bed thinking she was determined to get the whole story from Ramsey. If not Ramsey, then one of his brothers or cousins would do. Before leaving today Zane Westmoreland had tipped his hat at her, given her a flirty smile and a promise that he would be showing up for breakfast in the morning.

She shook her head. The only Westmoreland she wanted to concentrate on at the moment was the one who was probably sleeping peacefully in the bed only a few doors down the hall.

Six

"Good morning."

Ramsey glanced up from reading the morning's newspaper to stare into Chloe's face and immediately wished he hadn't. Her dark eyes looked slumberous and sensuously drowsy. A part of him was tempted to suggest that she forget about preparing breakfast for his men and go back to bed…but only if she would take him with her.

The muscles in his neck tightened at the very thought and he forced out his response. "Morning."

She sniffed the air. "Great, you've made coffee!"

He watched as she quickly headed toward the coffeepot. Today she was wearing another cute short dress with a pair of leggings underneath. He frowned. Did she have a pair of those things for every day of the week? And a different color for every day?

He took a sip of his coffee and watched as she poured hers,

adding cream and sugar into the mix before leaning against the counter and taking what looked like a much-needed sip.

"Excellent," she said.

"Thanks." Was she smiling? And if she was, then what the heck for? Could a cup of coffee first thing in the morning do that to her? As far as he could recall she'd been barely speaking to him when they'd parted yesterday afternoon. And why did knowing he'd contributed to putting that smile on her face send a good feeling vibrating through him? Damn.

He gazed back down at his newspaper. To be honest, he was hoping that he would have been in and out of the kitchen this morning before she'd gotten up. He was determined more so than ever to put distance between them. Maybe then he'd be able to get a good night's sleep.

"I'm doing omelets this morning. Would you like to go ahead and place your order?"

He glanced over at her. She was opening cabinets pulling out bowls, pots and pans. Had she said omelets? The last time he'd eaten an omelet was when he'd gone on a business trip and stayed at a hotel. It had been delicious.

"Yes, please," he said, trying to keep the excitement out of his voice. "I'd like that."

"How would you like it?"

He fought back the urge not to say the first thing that came into his mind, which would have given away his lusty thoughts. Hell, it was too early to think about that kind of stuff. But then, early morning sex wasn't so bad. And he had a feeling she would be able to cook in the bedroom with just as much heat as she used in the kitchen.

It took him only a few minutes to fill her in on the ingredients he wanted in his omelet. She nodded and went right to work. He watched her as she added the onions, green peppers, tomatoes…

Ramsey's mouth began watering. For both the omelet and for her. Moving around the kitchen, she was a sight to see. And he felt the lower part of his body getting there. The huge bulge behind his zipper wasn't a joke.

"What about a glass of orange juice?"

He blinked, realized he'd been staring. "Thanks. That will work."

At the moment he couldn't think of many things that wouldn't work, especially if she were to place her hands on it. Shivers went through him when he thought of places she could place her hands…on him.

She crossed the room and placed the plate on the table, right in front of him, and a glass of OJ beside his plate. "Thanks."

She smiled. "No problem."

He began eating while thinking it might not be a problem for her, but it was definitely becoming one for him. He didn't look up when she refilled his cup of coffee. "Thanks."

"Sure."

He took his time to savor the meal which deserved all the savoring it could get. The omelet was simply delicious. He liked glancing up every once in a while to watch as she fried bacon and cooked sausage. In no time at all the smell of breakfast was all over his kitchen.

And he noted she had come out of her shoes. She had kicked them in a corner and was gliding around the kitchen in her bare feet. He smiled as he glanced down at her toes again and felt his breathing come out slow and easy.

They hadn't said a word over the past thirty minutes. He was satisfied in letting her do her thing, and evidently she had no problem in letting him eat in peace while he finished reading the newspaper.

With the newspaper read and his plate clean, he decided to strike up a conversation. There were some things about her that he needed to know. "Do you have any family around these parts, Chloe?"

Chloe kept her attention trained on what she was doing, refusing to let the sound of Ramsey's deep, throaty voice wreak havoc on her mind. It was bad enough she could inhale his masculine scent over that of the bacon frying. That might sound like a lot of bull to some, but she was convinced it was true, which was the reason her nipples felt so sensitive. Bacon would not have caused that effect.

"No. I don't have family around these parts," she said, wondering why he'd asked.

"So you relocated here?"

"Yes."

"Without knowing anyone?"

She wondered how she could answer that without telling an outright lie. "Not exactly. I have a girlfriend from college who lives here and decided to give this area a try."

He nodded. "So you're living with your girlfriend?"

Her answer to that would not be a lie. "Yes, when I'm not staying here as your cook."

He pushed his plate aside and leaned back in his chair. "So where are you from?"

She forced a smile as she glanced over at him. "Where do you think I'm from?"

"Somewhere in the South."

"Yes, I'm from Florida, more specifically Tampa."

Deciding she had answered enough questions, Chloe resolved it was her turn to ask a few. "So, what happened with Raphael and his five wives? I didn't think a divorce was that easy back in the day."

Ramsey shrugged. "During our research we discovered the first woman he ran off with was a preacher's wife. He couldn't marry her because she was already married."

Chloe lifted a brow. "Then why did he run off with her?"

"To save her from an abusive marriage. And before you ask, the second wife he took off her husband's hands, with her husband's blessing, to save a possible scandal."

Ramsey decided that was all he would tell her for now. It was just enough to keep her curious. Why he was baiting her he really wasn't sure. Maybe the reason was that he liked seeing the look of interest in her eyes.

He stood and carried his plate, coffee cup and glass over to the sink.

"You don't have to do that," she said.

"Yes, I do. I was raised to clean up after myself."

And just like yesterday, when he reached the sink she deliberately moved out of his way. Knowing she was trying to avoid his touch bothered him. He reached out and grabbed hold of her hand. She glanced over at him, startled.

"Why are you afraid of me, Chloe?" It was then that he realized he was running his fingers up and down her arm.

She lifted her chin, but did not try pulling her hand away. "What makes you think I'm afraid of you?"

"You're trying to avoid me."

She lifted a haughty brow. "I could very well say the same thing about you, Ramsey."

That was true, he thought to himself. Instead of denying it, he was silent for a moment. And when he felt a shudder pass through her from the way he was running his fingers up her arms he locked his gaze to hers.

"Why the hell do we let this keep happening to us?" he asked in a low, throaty tone.

Surprisingly, she gave him a faint smile. "Hey, you're the one who was trying to work me out of your system."

He nodded. "With yesterday's kiss," he replied.

"Yes."

Now it was his time to smile. "It didn't work."

She shrugged. "Maybe your heart just wasn't in it."

His smile quickly transformed to a frown. "Like hell. Everything I had was in it."

She seemed to consider his words for half a second. "I know," she said, and sighed in dismay.

With his free hand he took his finger and tilted her chin. "But just to be sure, I think I should at least try it again. Yesterday didn't seem to work."

He then lowered his head and caught her lips in a drugging kiss, deliberately making it hot from the start. His tongue slid into her mouth on a breathless sigh and from there it was on. He deepened the kiss, devouring her mouth with a hunger that made yesterday's kiss seem tame.

He heard her moan. He felt the way the pebbled tips of her breasts were rubbing against his chest as if he wasn't even wearing a shirt. And once again, her stance was perfect to cradle his erection, which was hard as a rock, engorged, as aroused as a male shaft could get.

And just like yesterday, she was returning his kiss, lick for lick. Feasting on his mouth with just as much greed as he was feasting on hers. What was it about her taste, her flavor, the way their mouths fit together? His tongue seemed at home wrapped around hers.

He tried doing a mental calculation in his head, trying to figure out just how many steps it would take to reach the table. There he would strip her naked and...

The clearing of multiple throats had him reluctantly breaking contact with Chloe's mouth, but not before getting one final lick of his tongue across her lips. He lifted his head to glare over at the four men standing in his kitchen doorway with smirks on their faces.

It was Callum, Zane, Derringer and Jason. Of course it was Zane who had the damn nerve to ask, "Could you explain to us why you keep kissing your cook?"

Chloe eased her body into the sudsy water. Now it was late afternoon and everyone, including Ramsey, was gone and she intended to take time for herself. And she intended to get in bed early so she could be well-rested in the morning, now that she knew the routine.

She closed her eyes and thought about the events of the day, beginning that morning when the four men had walked in on her and Ramsey. This time instead of being embarrassed by the intrusion, she had been downright annoyed. And of course Ramsey had done just what she'd expected. He had begun avoiding her again.

He hadn't shown up for lunch. Instead he had locked himself in his office. Then around two o'clock, he left and he had yet to return and it was close to six. She had prepared dinner for him again and had left it warming in the oven. She had even sat on the sofa like yesterday, anticipating his return. But when it became evident he was staying away, she decided to take a bath, make a few calls and then get into bed early.

Thinking she had remained in the bathtub long enough, she stood to dry off with the huge towel. Everything for tomorrow was taken care of, so there was no reason for her to leave her bedroom tonight. She could use her PDA to check for any messages and to call and chat with her dad.

She paused when she thought she heard a car door slam, which meant Ramsey had returned home. Slipping into her robe and tying the sash tightly around her waist, she strolled over to the window and looked out. Ramsey was getting out of his truck.

She felt her body's reaction at seeing him. And as if he felt her presence, he tipped his head back and glanced up and saw her standing at the window.

Chloe sucked in a steadying breath the moment their eyes met. For a long time they just stood there, seemingly transfixed while staring at each other. And the heat of his gaze, the intensity of his stare touched her in areas that hadn't been touched in a long time.

She actually felt her body tremble at the desire building inside her and the feelings that clawed in her stomach from his unwavering gaze. No height or distance could stop the flow of sensations that were seeping into her every pore. And as she stood there all she could do was remember how he had taken her mouth for two days straight in hard, hungry and demanding kisses.

Unable to handle the intensity of his gaze or the passion he was stirring within her any longer, she drew in a deep breath before stepping away from the window.

Chloe fought the urge to rush downstairs and meet him at the door, to throw her arms around him and lift her mouth up to him, to be bold enough to take his mouth with the same intensity that he'd taken hers with earlier that day. She shook her head knowing there was no way she could or would do such a thing.

Removing her robe, she slipped into her pj's, deciding to

stick with her original plan to remain in her room for the rest of the evening. She and Ramsey might be under the same roof, but the less time they spent together, the better. And she had a good reason for feeling that way. She was getting drawn to him in a way that was more emotional than physical. She wished she could blame what she was feeling on irrational hormones but she knew that wasn't the case. Something else was taking place and she didn't want to think what that something could possibly be.

She felt vulnerable around him, like he could be the one man who could pull her into him so much that she would forget about herself. Daren had tried and failed. But a part of her knew if Ramsey took a mind to doing so that he would be successful. He had the ability to break through all the emotional walls she'd erected since her breakup with Daren.

With Ramsey she could feel herself losing her sense of will, her sense of logic and her common sense. There was something about him that was making her think things that she shouldn't. Like a little girl with those same set of dark eyes or a son with Ramsey's smile. She would admit right then and there if she was interested in a serious involvement with a man, he would head the list. And that worried her.

Ramsey opened the door to his home and leaned against it for a moment. He was fully aroused. The last thing he had expected when he'd pulled into his yard was to get out of his truck and participate in mind sex. He had stood there staring at Chloe while his entire mind had partaken in the most erotic fantasy possible. There was no part of him that had not been stimulated.

Through the window he could tell she was wearing a robe and he figured she was naked underneath. The thought of a naked Chloe had made him hard. Desire had surged through him in a way that it had never done before. While standing there staring at her he'd actually felt every muscle in his body tighten.

He glanced up at the stairs knowing the object of his desire, his red-hot passion and his erotic fantasies was up there behind closed doors. He was tempted, boy was he tempted, to go right up those stairs, knock on her door and kiss her in a way that would make the kiss they'd shared that morning seem like child's play. And now that her taste was embedded onto his tongue, he wanted more of it, doubted he would be able to get enough.

He rubbed his hand down his face wondering what in the hell was wrong with him. He had been around beautiful women before. For a while his sisters, who felt he'd still been hurting over Danielle's betrayal, had tried their hands at matchmaking. But no woman had held his interest until now. He was finding it hard to resist her. She was temptation at its very best. And on top of everything else, he was feeling emotions that he couldn't quite identify. The woman was bewitching him.

He had remained in his office the majority of the day, but all it took was to hear the laughter and the excitement in the voices of his men when they'd arrived at lunch to know that once again Chloe had made their day. That point was proven when he'd checked the shearing records for today. More sheep than normal had been sheared. Hell, they had basically set a record. That meant there was a connection between their cheerful attitudes and the work they did. A happy employee produced more and for the past two days his men had produced. And when he had dropped by the shearing plant this evening, right before closing time, he could hear the excitement in their voices when they talked about breakfast in the morning. After the omelets their anticipation as to what tomorrow morning would bring was evident.

He drew in a deep breath and it was at that moment he picked up the smell of something delicious. Pushing away from the door, he crossed the room to the kitchen and saw that Chloe had prepared his dinner again. He lifted the pots and checked the oven. She had made baked chicken, field peas, rice and gravy, and macaroni and cheese. A real Southern meal, something a westerner like him could appreciate. He had acquired a taste for Southern cuisine after meeting the Atlanta Westmorelands.

Deciding he would wash up for dinner, he moved toward the bathroom thinking he had deliberately stayed away today. That kiss he and Chloe had shared had shredded his senses, making resisting her nearly impossible. It was already rumored by his men that he had the hots for her and he didn't want to give them any more to talk about or speculate on. So leaving here for a while had been the decision that he'd made.

And then he'd had to deal with the ribbing from his brothers, Jason and Callum. Trying to convince them that Chloe was nothing more than his cook was beginning to sound lame even to his ears. He had walked away from them when he saw they were intent on drawing their own conclusions about his and Chloe's relationship, and he'd made a point not to accept their invitation for a game of poker over at Jason's place.

Luckily for him Dillon and Pamela had returned to town for a few days for Dillon to attend a business meeting, so he'd had the chance to visit with them. The newly married couple divided their time between here and Pamela's home in Gamble, Wyoming, because one of Pamela's sisters was in her last year of high school.

Dillon seemed extremely happy as a married man and Ramsey was happy for him. From the time he could remember, he and Dillon had been closer than just cousins. In essence, they were best friends and when their parents had perished in that plane crash, he had more than supported Dillon's desire to keep the family together.

Because Dillon was the oldest by some months, he had become head of the family and guardian for everyone. But the two of them had worked hard. It hadn't been easy raising their siblings and cousins, nine of whom had been under the age of sixteen.

Now all of them were over twenty-one, either in college or working alongside Dillon at Blue Ridge Land Development, the company that the two Westmoreland brothers—his father and Dillon's—had formed many years ago. Under Dillon's guidance, Blue Ridge was now a multimillion dollar company well known in the Mountain States. It employed over a thousand people. Every family member had worked there at some point in their lives before pursuing their dreams and other ambitions.

An hour later Ramsey had finished eating and was still licking his lips. The meal had been delicious. Chloe hadn't come downstairs and in a way he hadn't expected her to. She was well aware, just like he was, that something was taking place between them and it was something neither of them wanted. So it would be best to avoid the situation by avoiding each other. The attraction between them was too strong, the passion was too thick. And she was becoming his weakness. If he didn't get things in check, the desire he felt for her would consume him and that was something he simply refused to let happen.

He shook his head as he moved toward the stairs and the

moment he lifted his leg to take a step he inhaled her scent. It was the scent of a woman he wanted. Her fragrance was emitting from behind closed doors, drenching the air, teasing his nostrils and making him even more aroused. He hadn't gotten much sleep last night and he doubted things would be any better tonight.

When he reached the landing, he worked his shoulders to relieve the tension that had built there. Drawing in a heated breath he made it down the hall, forcing one foot in front of the other, intent on passing Chloe's door without stopping.

Easier said than done. When he reached her door he couldn't help but pause. He even raised his hand to knock before snatching it back to his side.

What the hell was happening to him?

He forced himself away from her door and quickly moved down the hall toward his own. He had to formulate a plan, at least until the weekend. Hopefully, she would leave those two days to go back to her own place, get her mail, water her plants, check in with her neighbors or whatever else she needed to do. By then they would need the distance. They would need the space. The weekend was three days away and he hoped like hell that he could hold out until then.

Seven

"So what do you think of Derringer?"

Chloe couldn't stop the smile from touching her lips. This was the third time this weekend that Lucia had asked that same question. "I told you twice already, but I'll tell you again," she teased, as she pulled off her jacket. "He is a very handsome man. I like him. He, Zane and Jason come by for breakfast and lunch quite a bit. They're nice guys. Big teasers."

She saw the wistful look in Lucia's eyes. They had just returned from having dinner together after going to a movie. "You know how you can make yourself known, don't you?"

Lucia rolled her eyes. "I know how *you* would make yourself known to him, Clo. You go after whatever it is that you want. You're daring. I'm not."

Chloe placed her hands on her hips. "So what are you going to do, Lou? Wait another year or so for him to need more paint thinner and hope you're in your father's store when he does?"

Lucia dropped down on her sofa with a downhearted look on her face. "Of course not." She then looked up at Chloe. "Enough about me since I refuse to have a pity party. How close are you to getting Ramsey to do the magazine cover and interview?"

Chloe shook her head and dropped down beside Lucia, looking just as downhearted. "It's not going well. Ramsey is avoiding me like the plague."

"Why?"

Chloe smiled over at her friend. "Too much sexual chemistry in the air when we're within ten feet of each other."

"Must be nice."

Chloe leaned back against the sofa and closed her eyes thinking that in essence it *should* be nice, but it wasn't. Ramsey made an appearance only when he had to. He got up each morning for his cup of coffee while she prepared breakfast and instead of hanging around, he took his breakfast and coffee into his office, claiming he had a lot of work to do. He came out for lunch to eat with his men, said very little and only stayed long enough to eat and leave. In the evenings, although she prepared dinner for him each evening, he usually stayed away until he was sure she was in bed.

He hadn't been home when she'd left to come here for the weekend. She had left a note on the kitchen table letting him know she would be returning Sunday evening. She had left her cell number in case something came up and she needed to be reached.

A smile touched her lips. Who was she kidding? She was hoping he would contact her for any reason and that wasn't good.

"Okay, Clo, you've gotten quiet on me. Open those eyes and tell me what's going on."

Chloe slowly opened her eyes to gaze over into Lucia's curious ones. She had an idea what was going on, but to say it out loud would be speaking it into existence and she wasn't ready to do that yet. There was no way she could tell Lucia that she might not be the only woman who'd fallen for a Westmoreland man.

"Stop being a worry wart. Nothing is going on." Chloe drew in a breath thinking that Lucia had no idea just how true that was. Nothing was really going on. She was no closer to getting Ramsey to agree to that cover or an interview than before she'd shown up. Somehow, she had to get him to stop avoiding her, sexual chemistry or no sexual chemistry. And if she were to come clean now and tell him the truth, he would probably kick her off his land so fast it would make her head spin.

She stood, not ready for Lucia to question her further about anything. "It's late and I think I'll turn in early."

"I think I'll turn in as well. Mom and Dad invited us to dinner after church tomorrow and then later Aunt Pauline wants us to drop by her place."

"All right and then after that I need to return to the Westmoreland place." This would be her last week and she needed to make some kind of headway.

Later that night as Chloe lay in bed, images of Ramsey flowed through her mind. Two days ago while preparing lunch she had glanced out the window in time to see a shirtless Ramsey carrying a lamb in his arms across the yard to the barn. With jeans riding low on his hips she had stared at his physique, taking in every inch of his tight abs, strong arms and tight buns. He was the only man alive who could literally make her drool.

And if that wasn't bad enough, the following morning at breakfast when he'd sat with his men, she saw again how well he got along with them as well as his brothers and cousin.

She shifted in bed admitting she missed him. She missed the ranch. And as crazy as it sounded, she even missed preparing food for the men. They were so appreciative and complimentary.

She closed her eyes thinking of Ramsey and knowing she would be glad to see him tomorrow when she returned to the ranch.

Ramsey pushed back the curtain and looked out, something he'd done too many times over the past hour. Where was she? The note she'd left on the kitchen table said she would return Sunday evening. In his part of the world the evening time came well before ten at night. The last time he had glanced at the clock it was heading toward the eleventh hour.

She had left her phone number, but he had thrown it away, refusing to be tempted to call her and now he was worried. What if something had happened. He had no way of reaching her and had no idea just where she lived in the city.

It had rained earlier and the road off the main highway leading to Westmoreland Country was known to be slippery after a storm. He let the curtain slip back in place and began pacing the floor again. At that moment he realized just how little he knew about Chloe, other than she was the woman who aroused him to no end.

This was crazy. He'd let a woman in his house to cook for his men, sleep in his guestroom, use his washer and dryer to wash her bed linens before she'd taken off for the weekend, and all he knew about her was her name.

Okay, he knew a little bit more about her than that. He knew she was a hell of a cook and beautiful as beautiful could get. He knew she had a hell of a body, although he was yet to see her bare legs. He knew she got along with his men and had cooked a huge chocolate cake last week when Colin Lawrence had turned fifty.

He also knew what she did to him whenever she looked at him for any length of time. Truth was, although he wished like hell he didn't have to admit it, in one short week he'd discovered a taste unlike any he'd ever sampled before, and her scent was one hell of a fragrance, an aroma he could breathe into his nostrils for days. But she had managed to do something no other woman had been capable of doing in ten years.

She had ignited his passion.

He wanted to know how it felt to lose himself inside her, to feel her heat, have her body, legs and all, wrapped all around him, feel his erection swell to the fullest size possible inside her, and be as greedy for her breasts as he was for her mouth.

His hands clenched into fists at his side. He was the Westmoreland, so he'd been told, who had the least amount of charm. The one who didn't need sex as often as the rest to maintain a normal life. Yet here he was with his heart thumping like crazy in his chest as he imagined doing all kinds of naughty things to Chloe. For the first time in hell knows when, he was thinking about getting laid. Bottom line, he was horny as hell.

The unwanted direction of his thoughts no longer shocked him. Instead what it did was propel him to want to do more than think about it. He wanted to act on it and let the chips fall where they may. He wanted…

His thoughts were suddenly interrupted by the sound of a vehicle pulling up. Quickly crossing the room he glanced out the window and saw it was Chloe returning. He frowned as he dropped the curtain back in place. She was late.

He dismissed the feeling of relief knowing she was all right and was filled with anger. The least she could have done was call to let him know she would be late. Standing across the room he faced the door with his arms over his chest. She had a lot of explaining to do. The nerve of her to make him worry for nothing.

Her scent filled the air the moment the door opened, but in anger he chose to ignore it. But when she walked over his threshold wearing a white blouse and a short denim skirt— with no leggings underneath—that showed the most beautiful pair of legs he had ever seen, he gritted his teeth knowing there was no way he could ignore them.

Chloe closed the door behind her, saw Ramsey standing across the room glaring and quickly knew she was so not ready for this. In fact, she had decided to wait before returning in hopes that he would be in bed already. She tried to ignore how good he looked. The man wore a pair of jeans like they'd been made just for his body. They fit snug, showing impressive hard thighs and tight abs. Another thing she noticed was that it looked as if he hadn't shaved since she'd left. The stubble look suited him. It made him look even sexier in a sinful sort of way.

Trying to take her mind off his ultra-fine body, she stared back at him, wondering what his problem was. She had left everything in perfect order before she'd headed into town for the weekend. She had even washed and dried her bed linens, although he'd mentioned he had a housekeeper who came every Saturday morning to clean and do laundry. And why was he staring at her legs like he'd never seen a pair of legs before? Her skirt was short, but it wasn't that short. She'd worn some shorter. If he was about to tell her there was something wrong with her outfit, that it wasn't appropriate to wear on his ranch, then she would let him have it.

Deciding to just get this over with and give just as good as she got, she lifted her chin, glared back at him and asked, "Ramsey, is there a problem?"

Ramsey's gut clenched and his jaw tightened. Her legs were long and shapely. They were the kind that looked perfect in a short dress from the top of her thighs all the way down to her ankles.

"Ramsey, I asked was there a problem?" she asked testily.

His gaze moved from her legs to her face. "You're late."

What on earth did he mean by that? Chloe wondered as a confused frown covered her face. She must have heard him wrong. "Excuse me?"

"I said you're late. Your note said you would be returning Sunday evening and it's almost eleven."

She dropped her overnight bag by her feet. "And what of it? I'm not on a time clock. In fact, I am not even working for you today. As long as I'm here to prepare breakfast in the morning what business is it of yours?"

Ramsey stiffened. She had asked a good question. What business was it of his? He then said the first thing that came to his mind. "This is my house."

She seemed taken aback by that response. "Are you standing here telling me that I have a curfew?"

Was that what he was saying? He shook his head. "No, you don't have a curfew, but since you left a note saying you would be returning in the evening, at least you could have had the decency to call."

Her gaze locked on his face. *Decency?* Blood rushed through her veins as anger consumed her. He had the gall to utter such a word? She crossed the room to him. "Let's talk about decency, Ramsey. If you would have had the *decency* to be here when I left instead of avoiding me like I have the pox, I would not have had to leave that note."

Ramsey was taken aback by Chloe's anger. As far as he was concerned she didn't have a damn thing to be angry about. She hadn't been the one who'd endured sleepless nights knowing she was just down the hall from him when the need to bury himself deep inside her had nearly driven him insane. Hell, if only she knew that the reason he'd deliberately made himself scarce most of last week was because anytime he saw her he got an automatic erection that wouldn't go down.

Furthermore, he was sick and tired of finding places to go in the afternoons just so he wouldn't be tempted to make one of those erotic dreams he'd had over the past week come true. Tired of unexplainable emotions, escalated hormones and a frantic urge to make love to her until neither of them had an ounce of energy left.

He took a step closer as his anger level moved up another notch. "You don't get it do you?" he asked in a voice that was rough, close to the edge. "I stayed away to do us both a favor, Chloe. Had I been here you would never have walked out that door."

The hard, cold reality was that he was a lit piece of dynamite ready to explode, preferably inside her. Point blank, he wanted her in a way he'd never wanted any woman and with a need that was pushing him over the edge and he was determined to take her right with him.

He could tell by her expression she hadn't liked what he'd said. She took a step closer, got in his face, put her mouth just inches from his, their noses almost touched. "Ha! And just what were you going to do? Tie me up?"

A slow smile slid over his lips. If only she knew how many times such a thought had crossed his mind. He'd never been into that bondage stuff, but he could just imagine such a thing with her. "Considering the state I've been in all week, the state I happen to be in right now, tying you up would have definitely been an option."

Chloe stared at him, stunned at his admission, and at that moment she realized not only what he'd said but what he'd meant. Somewhere along the line their conversation had become sexual. Maybe for him it had always been that way, but due to her raging anger she had failed to see it. However, she was seeing it now. She could feel his heat and that heat was being passed on to her. Even the distended nipples pressing against her blouse felt like they were ready to detonate. And the area between her legs, more specifically the depths of her womb, felt hot.

"And do you know what I would have done after tying you up, Chloe?"

Nibbling on her bottom lip she held his gaze while her entire body felt like a bonfire. She'd never considered herself a fiercely passionate woman, but at that moment the raw images going through her mind, of her bound to his bed, legs spread, with him naked and crawling over her, to mate with her, had her speechless.

He didn't wait for her to respond to his question. "I would have stripped you naked and then licked you all over from head to toe."

Added to the very image flowing in her mind, she could

definitely see him doing that. A heated ache settled between her thighs and when she felt her panties get wet she tightened her legs together. Hot passion, deep desire was taking over her entire body with his words and every part of her was responding, without any restraints.

"But do you know where my mouth would have lingered, Chloe? Where it would have devoured you to the fullest, given you the most sensual pleasure?"

When she didn't say anything, he leaned in, whispered close to her ear and what he said, as well as the erotic picture his words made, had her weak in the knees. And it didn't help matters that she could feel the warmth of his breath against her neck.

"And trust me, you aren't out of the woods yet," he said in a deep, husky and sexually-laden voice. "So if you don't want me with the same intensity that I want you, with the same intensity that I plan on taking you, then I suggest you walk out that door right now, because I refuse to avoid you any longer."

Chloe swallowed tightly while admitting inwardly that she wanted him, wanted him to take her and with the same intensity he was alluding to. There was no way she could or would deny that. And she knew that standing before her was a fiercely passionate man. She had known it from the first time she had seen him that day crossing the street. There had been something about him that had sent a sensual thrill through her, had made her entirely aware of him as a woman. It had made her fantasize about him every night since then. So what he was threatening to do stimulated her more than he would ever know.

But then at the same time, he was giving her an out without having to feel guilty about leaving him in a tough spot in regard to losing a cook. She should take it. But the bottom line was that she didn't want to take it. She wanted to take him instead.

"Chloe?"

Her name flowed from his lips in a deeply throaty tone. She met his gaze. "Yes?"

"I'm waiting."

She inhaled deeply, took a couple of steps to him, flattened her hands against his chest, looked up into his eyes and then told him calmly, "So am I."

Ramsey's self-control snapped and the speed in which his mouth swept down on Chloe's had his head spinning. But the twirling stopped and was replaced by an explosion going off in his skull the moment his tongue was planted firmly in her mouth.

She tasted like the strawberry cake she had baked on Thursday and he was tempted to eat her mouth with the same greediness with which he'd consumed that slice of cake. And when his tongue began lapping her up, savoring every inch of her mouth, exploring every nook and cranny, he heard the moan that escaped from her throat. Her delicious taste consumed him, went to his head, speared every part of his body and enflamed his senses.

And he still wanted to draw her deeper into himself.

The hard throbbing of his erection was letting him know that kissing her would not be enough. His control was eroding and taking his sanity right along with it, while at the same time his hunger was being escalated. And his body, every nerve ending, every cell, was demanding to be fed. He suddenly pulled his mouth away, needing more. And needing it now.

"Ramsey?"

Her voice was soft, her breath hot, and the sound of his

name from her lips was as sweet as her taste. He knew at that moment he had to remove her clothes and the thought of taking off that skirt and getting between those legs sent a shudder through every part of him.

He knew there was no way he could make it up the stairs to his bedroom. The sofa would have to do. It was sturdy and strong which was a good thing because she was in for a hard ride. He had given her fair warning, but she hadn't taken it. Soon enough she would discover just what she had unleashed.

The air surrounding them was thick with sexual tension. The rush of sensations that were pounding through his veins and making his insides quiver, drove him to reach out and draw her back close to him. His hands began moving, roaming all over her and lifting her short skirt to touch the backside he enjoyed looking at so much.

He felt her shiver in his arms, heard her say his name again and with the sound of the hunger he heard in her voice, more than ever before, consumed him. He needed to kiss her again, let his tongue stroke inside her mouth while his hands stroked her flesh.

That wasn't enough.

Suddenly, his hands went to her blouse, his fingers gripped the fabric and with one hard tug ripped it from her body.

Chloe gasped and when she saw the intensity of desire that burned in Ramsey's eyes she knew her blouse was just the beginning. He proved her right when his hands reached for her bra. Blood surged through her veins when he opened the front clasp, freeing her breasts, but not for long.

After pulling the bra off her shoulders and tossing it aside, he took the twin mounds in his hands as if testing their softness and shaping their fullness. And then he lowered his mouth to capture a puckered nipple into his hot mouth. The moment his tongue touched the tip, sucked it deep, she dug her nails into his shoulders as sensations ripped through her. Intense pleasure trailed not far behind and caused her nipples to harden even more.

"Ramsey…" She whispered his name, barely able to stand on her feet any longer as he attacked her breasts with his mouth like a starving man.

Instead of answering, with his mouth still on her breasts, he moved his hands downward to raise her skirt. His fingers found the crotch of her panties. The moment he touched the drenched spot she moaned, but not before she heard his rough growl. He pulled back, released her breasts and gripped her skirt to pull it down her hips.

Within seconds she was standing in front of him wearing nothing more than wet panties. He took a step back to remove his shirt, popping buttons in his haste, before stripping it from his shoulders. His naked chest was perfect and she couldn't help moving, closing the distance and reaching out to rake her nails across the hard, muscled hairy chest, liking the feel beneath her fingertips.

He captured her hand and holding her gaze he began licking her fingers, one by one. His tongue felt hot against her sensitive flesh and she shuddered when sensations tore through her.

"You like that?" His voice was heavy, deep, sexy.

She could only nod.

"You enjoy my tongue on you?"

"Yes," she whispered, barely able to get out the single word.

"Good, now let's see how you enjoy my tongue *in* you."

He eased down in front of her and holding her hips he leaned forward, pressed his nose against the crotch of her panties, as if to inhale her scent. And then he flicked out his tongue and it felt blazing hot against the silky material. Pleasure eased over her and she felt on the verge of exploding.

Ramsey leaned back and looked up to hold her gaze as he began easing her panties down her legs. When she stepped out of them he could only lean farther back on his haunches and look at her up and down, fighting hard to breathe while doing so.

He was mesmerized. Her legs seemed endless. They were beautiful, shapely, alluring. They were silky smooth and should never be covered with a pair of leggings again. Unable to hold out any longer, he reached out and touched her legs, stroked them up and down, front and back, the pad of his fingers reveling in the feel of her skin. These were legs that were making him harder just looking at them. Legs he wanted wrapped around him tight, holding him inside her body while he thrust in and out of her.

But first, he had to taste her.

Leaning in closer his hands slid to her hips as he angled his mouth to her center. Instinctively, she parted her thighs and when he gently opened her up and his tongue delved inside her, she clung to him to hold on, which to him was a good thing.

His tongue swiped at her a couple of times before going for the gusto, stroking her, licking her and sucking with an intensity he felt all the way to the exquisitely painful tip of his erection. She began moving against his mouth and he gripped her hips tighter to hold her steady and then his hands shifted and went to her rump, gripping it and pushing her closer to his mouth, while at the same time he lifted her legs off the floor to wrap around his shoulders, cupping her backside in the palms of his hands for support. Keeping his mouth locked to her his tongue was having a field day, licking her into pleasure, deliberately searing her senses. She clenched her hands to the side of his head, moaned his name over and over. And then she began to shudder. He felt it. He tasted it. And he didn't intend to remove his mouth from her until he'd gotten his fill.

Moments later he pulled his mouth away, untangled her legs from around his shoulders and eased her down with him to the floor. He glanced over at her and licked his lips. "Delicious," he whispered in a throaty voice.

She had been more than delicious. She was incredible. The taste and heat of her was still on his tongue. At that moment, something inside him snapped. The need to join his body with hers was monumental.

He released a growl before he shifted his body, capturing her mouth the moment he could do so. He was going to take her, give them both pleasure, have them exploding all over the place, and his erection throbbed violently in anticipation.

He couldn't get out of his jeans quickly enough and she didn't help matters when she began nipping on his shoulders, as if branding him hers. *Hers.* A groan left his chest when she bit down and he stared at her. She gave him one hell of a naughty smile not the least regretful. "I'm going to make you pay for that," he promised in a deep voice. With that said, he kicked his jeans away and pulled her to him.

"Condom?"

"Damn." Her mention of protection made him realize just how over the edge he was and the risk he had been about to take. Looking around for his jeans he quickly found them and fumbled through the pockets until he located his wallet. He found a condom packet, not wanting to think just how long it had been in there and hoping like hell it would still be effective.

Ripping open the packet he quickly sheathed himself knowing her eyes were glued to him and watching every move he made. When he was finished, he went back to her, pulled her into his arms and kissed her deeply, hungrily and wildly.

He hadn't expected this. He hadn't expected a need erupting inside him so intense that he felt driven to make love to her in a way he hadn't ever made love to a woman before. She was demanding something from him, pulling it out effortlessly and he knew the only way he would be totally satisfied was when he was embedded deeply inside of her.

He pulled his mouth from hers, reveling in a need so intense he was goaded into immediate action. She was so responsive, filled with as much passion as he was feeling and he wanted her now. He shifted their bodies to place her beneath him, pressing her back on the rug. Ramsey spread her legs with his knee. Gripping her hips tight in his hands, he surged inside of her, going deep, all the way to the hilt.

He watched her eyes widen at the intrusion and when he began moving, thrusting inside of her, her gaze became filled with a pleasure that touched his soul and made his erection throb even more inside of her.

Her heat surrounded him. Her muscles clenched him, pulled everything out of him; made pleasure build inside of him, gather in his shaft, and he felt snug inside of her, like it was where he belonged.

He began moving harder. Going faster. Thrusting deeper. And when he called out her name the sound detonated like a bomb. He exploded at the same moment she did. Pleasure ripped through them both and he gripped her hips tighter as he drove even deeper inside of her.

"Chloe."

Her name was a guttural sound off his lips and he moved his hands from her hips to her hair as he filled her with his release. Shivers ran down his spine and he could only sigh as sensations filled him to capacity.

And when he eased up to take her mouth in his, he promised himself that sometime tonight, they would make it to the bedroom.

Eight

Sometime hours later, they made it to the bedroom. Barely. The most difficult part in getting there had been the stairs. Ramsey couldn't recall ever making love to anybody on stairs. He was a more traditional guy. But there had been nothing traditional about anything he and Chloe had done tonight, and even now as he lay flat on his back while she slept literally on top of him, he couldn't help but think about everything that had happened from the time Chloe had returned.

He'd been keyed up, part angry and part fighting an intense desire that had been eating away at him since the moment he first laid eyes on her. And when she had walked through the door tonight, and he'd seen her...and her bare legs, he had tried smothering his desire with anger by lashing out at her in a subject matter that really hadn't made any sense. That hadn't worked. And he was glad it hadn't. If she had taken the option to walk out that door, he probably would have died then and there. His need for her was so strong, so intense that even now he was getting hard all over again.

He was tempted to wake her but he would let her rest. She deserved every second that she slept. The woman was amazing and had more passion than he could ever imagine any woman having. She had met his every thrust and fueled his passion in a way that even now made him breathless. She had ridden him to the point of madness and it was only after their passion had exploded in a gigantic maelstrom that she had slumped down on top of him. She hadn't moved since.

He could only marvel at the soft body on top of him and even now their bodies were still intimately connected. He inhaled, taking in her scent. Her bare breasts pressing deep into his chest and her legs, those legs that had been his downfall earlier, were entwined in his. He closed his eyes to sleep awhile.

Ramsey wasn't sure just how long he'd slept, but when he lifted his lids it was to stare into a gorgeous pair of dark eyes. At the realization that she was awake, his body immediately became aroused. His erection jerked to life inside of her and from her expression he knew she felt it the moment he had.

He saw the rush of heat that inflamed her features and that same heat was there in the depths of the eyes staring down at him. Together they felt his shaft continue to expand inside of her, stretching her fully to accommodate him totally.

And when her muscles began clenching him, he knew it was time to start moving. But not until he was on top. She was the one who'd ridden the last go around and now it was his turn. He gritted his teeth as she continued to clench his hardness and to get control of his mind and senses. He began sliding his hand up and down her back, loving the feel of the soft texture of her skin. And then when he knew he had her absolute attention, he flipped her onto her back.

Surprise lit her eyes. "Hey! That's not fair."

Ramsey smiled, deciding he wouldn't waste time arguing with her, not when he wanted to make love to her, ride her, pump inside of her over and over again.

Automatically, she wrapped her legs around his waist and when she smiled up at him, he knew before it was all said and done, she was going to drain everything out of him. It was hard to believe they had already made love several times that night. In fact, except for the time he'd allowed her to sleep, they had made love nonstop.

When he pushed himself deeper inside of her, the groan that curled in her throat triggered something within him and he began moving, lifting up her hips to receive his strong strokes. His thrusts were fine-tuned, primitively precise and painstakingly deliberate.

"Ramsey." She moaned out his name over and over while thrashing her head back and forth against the bedcovers.

"Look at me, Chloe," he said in a guttural groan and when she did, and her eyes clashed with his, his grip tightened on her hips and what he saw in her gaze ignited something within him to the point where he felt consumed in fire, torched by desire. But he didn't stop. He continued going, moving in and out of her, needing her, wanting her and determined to consume her the way she was totally consuming him.

Chloe actually felt every muscle in her body, every single vein that ran through her, become electrified, gush with a need so extreme that she could only shiver, shudder in pleasure as Ramsey continued to drive deep and hard inside of her.

And when he leaned forward to capture her lips, she felt the sensations that started at her center, tear straight up her legs and went all the way to her toes. And like all the other times when they kissed, he took her mouth with a mastery that had her as responsive to a man as any woman could be. She wrapped her legs around him even tighter, locking him into her body.

She held tight to his shoulders, clung to him as he wrapped his tongue around hers while imitating the same rhythm of his thrusts below. She had never experienced passion this hot, this torrid, this out-of-body uncivilized. It was as if she was being sucked into a raging sea of unrestrained fervor, a heated craze that had her body literally begging for more, and she was showing him just how much more by the way she was lifting herself off the mattress to meet his every turbulent thrust.

She wanted this. She needed this. And the necessity of her desire had become essential, a crucial desperation. There was nothing trivial about the way she was feeling and when she suddenly felt herself tumbling headlong into an abyss of sensations that had her screaming his name, she shuddered straight into a climax that rocked her world. And when he finally let go of her mouth to throw his head back and let out a guttural growl, she was thrown off the edge all over again and together they went skyrocketing into another mind-blowing orgasm.

He tightened his hold on her, gripped more securely to her hips and locked their bodies into a bond of sensual fulfillment. She felt him totally and completely, and there was no part of her left untouched. Unconsumed. Not taken.

And when he leaned up to take her mouth again, she was very much aware of one major thing. He was breaking through her barriers and making her feel things that were emotional as well as physical. She had never intended for such a thing to happen. But it had, and as he continued to kiss her in a way that she felt all the way to her toes, he had proven that he *could* put a smile of satisfaction on her face all by himself.

Although he didn't plan for it to happen, Ramsey slept later than usual the next morning. It was only when he heard the sound of a man's laughter, namely his brother Zane's, that Ramsey realized he was in bed alone. He didn't recall Chloe getting out of it. Had exhaustion knocked him into a dead sleep? He'd never been a sound sleeper before and was known to be an early riser. But then he'd never had sex all night with a woman before either.

He slid out of bed. It was not his intent for Chloe to prepare breakfast alone and he had meant to help. It was the least he could do when his voracious sexual hunger had kept her up most of the night. Granted he wasn't an ace in the kitchen like she was, but he could at least follow directions.

Before heading for the bathroom for a quick shower he glanced over at the clock on the nightstand and frowned. It was just a little past four, so what the hell was Zane doing here already? And if Zane was here that meant so was Derringer and Jason because the three were thick as thieves. And he wouldn't be surprised if Callum wasn't downstairs, too. The four had shown up early one day last week. The day they had walked in on his kissing Chloe. It had been a second occurrence for his brothers and is what had prompted him to start putting distance between him and Chloe. A lot of good that did.

And as he stepped in the shower he did know one thing for certain: He wouldn't be putting distance between them any longer.

"Come on, Chloe, there's no way that brother of mine is still asleep. Ramsey wouldn't know how to sleep late even if it killed him," Zane was saying. He held his coffee cup midway to his lips, looked over at Chloe a little too long to suit her, before a smile touched his lips. "Unless…"

Instead of finishing what he was about to say, his smile widened as he took a sip of his coffee and then continued eating. Chloe was grateful for that although she wasn't sure what Zane Westmoreland was thinking at that moment. And she was grateful for the conversation going on between Jason, Derringer and Callum and the fact they hadn't heard Zane's comment. But because they knew Ramsey just as well as Zane, they had to be wondering the same thing. Why was he still in bed asleep?

She was beginning to feel uneasy. Had Zane or any of the others seen passion marks on her neck? Were they wondering why she was wearing a scarf of all things this morning? When she had eased out of bed careful to not wake Ramsey, and had gone back to her bedroom to take a shower, she had been appalled at all the marks Ramsey's stubble had made all over her body. And then there were some he had intentionally made. Specifically, the ones on her neck. It was as if he had been determined to mark her as his and the very thought of that sent shivers down her spine.

"About time you got out of bed, Ram. What are you? Sick or something?"

Chloe heard the smirk in Derringer's voice and turned to see that Ramsey had walked into the kitchen. He was wearing nothing but his jeans that hung low on his hips, and her breath stopped and her pulse leaped at the sight of his broad shoulders and bare chest. His feet were also bare and the thatch of dark hairs on his chest was damp, which indicated he'd just gotten out of the shower.

Ignoring his brothers, cousin and friend, his gaze was on

her and without acknowledging their presence he made his way to where she stood. Before she could finally release her breath, he leaned over and kissed her in front of them.

There was what seemed to be shocked silence in the room. At least she thought there was, but the only sure thing she knew at that moment was that he was kissing her in front an audience. It wasn't a long kiss, but if he'd intended to make a point, he most certainly had. And when he finally pulled his mouth away, she stared up into a face that was smiling in a way that showed both dimples.

"Good morning, Chloe."

If the kiss hadn't done her in, then his throaty and husky voice definitely would have. She forced herself to begin breathing normally and said, "Good morning, Ramsey."

With his arms still locked around her waist, he turned toward the four men sitting at his breakfast table. "Is there a reason the four of you feel you should be getting preferential treatment for breakfast? Especially when three of you aren't employed by me."

Zane smiled. "But we're family."

Ramsey nodded slowly. "Just make sure you remember that when dealing with Chloe in the future."

Derringer lifted a brow. "So that's how things are going to be from now on?"

"Yes," Ramsey said without a smile on his face. "That's how things are going to be from now on."

Chloe's eyes were glued to Ramsey as her gaze ran over him. Her attention was directed to him so much that she missed part of what he'd said to the others. All she knew was that when she glanced at the men, they were staring at her as if with new insight. Subconsciously, she reached for her scarf to adjust it around her neck, wondering if they were seeing far more than she wanted them to see.

Deciding the mood around her had turned much too serious, she pulled out of Ramsey's arms and said, "I suggest you go put on a shirt. I'm about to fry some more bacon and I'd hate for popping grease to hit you."

She saw the grin on his face and was almost taken back at how different his attitude was from last week. It was a vast improvement. Would one night of mind-blowing lovemaking do that to you? She would be one of the first to admit that whereas she should feel tired because of the brevity of sleep the night before, she felt renewed energy running through her body. Although she had to force herself out of bed, after having slept wrapped in Ramsey's arms, once she had begun moving around the kitchen she had actually felt rejuvenated.

"Thanks for the warning," he said, and leaning closer he placed a sensuous peck on her lips before strolling out of the kitchen. The swagger on his walk was enough to give any woman heart failure, while making her wonder just what he could do with that swaggering body beneath the sheets. She knew the answer to that firsthand and remnants of pleasure flowed through her body from the memory.

Pulling in a deep breath she glanced at the four men who were staring at her. They had become a bunch of regulars during breakfast and lunch, always arriving earlier than everyone to chat with her and with each other.

From their conversations she knew about the horse breeding and training business Zane, Derringer and Jason were about to embark on, as well as the fact that Callum was in no hurry to return to Australia, although she hadn't figured out why.

Clearing her throat, she asked, "Would any of you like anything else? More coffee?"

Before they could respond, she could hear vehicles pulling up in the yard. She was grateful her day was about to begin and welcomed the opportunity to stay busy.

"And you're sure without Zane, Derringer and Jason's spread that you'll still have enough land for your sheep to graze?" Dillon Westmoreland leaned back in the chair behind his desk to ask his cousin.

Ramsey didn't respond but looked as if he was lost in other thoughts. "Are you okay, Ram?"

Dillon's concerned question snapped Ramsey's attention back and he couldn't help but smile. "Yes, I'm okay."

After breakfast Ramsey decided to leave the house for a while, not to avoid Chloe, but to give her the time she needed to prepare for the noon hour. Had he remained he would have done everything he could have to get her back upstairs or better yet, he would have played his hand at enticing her into participating in a number of quickies. So trying to behave he had driven over to Shady Tree Ranch to spend time with Dillon and Pamela.

He could feel Dillon staring at him and looked up and met his gaze. "I understand things have turned somewhat serious between you and your cook, Ram."

Ramsey didn't have to wonder where Dillon had gotten that information. And today, Ramsey had no problem acknowledging that was true. Even when he had dated he'd never been into sex just for the sake of sex, which is why a casual relationship with a woman never appealed to him. And because he hadn't been in the market for a serious relationship either, he'd been satisfied to remain a loner. It was only when things with him got so bad and sexual needs got the best of him, that he would seek out female companionship for a night. But those times had been few and far between. Now he couldn't imagine not making love to Chloe on a regular basis, not waking up during the night with her beside him, their legs locked together, her delectable bottom curled up against him. His...

"Ram?"

He glanced up, realizing Dillon had caught him daydreaming again. "Yes?"

"You sure you're okay?"

Ram leaned back in his chair, deciding to be completely honest. "No, I don't know if I'm okay," he finally said. He studied Dillon thoughtfully. "I can recall the first time you mentioned to me about meeting Pamela. I could hear something in your voice."

Dillon chuckled. "Yes, and it was probably the same thing I could hear in yours that day you came over here and mentioned Chloe Burton was your temporary cook."

Ramsey was taken aback by Dillon's claim. "No way. I had just met the woman that day."

Dillon nodded. "And remember, I had just met Pam that day when I spoke to you on the phone as well."

Ramsey frowned, not sure he liked what Dillon was hinting at. He quickly stood up. "Trust me, Dillon, it's not that kind of party."

A smile curved the corners of Dillon's lips when he said, "I didn't think it was that kind of party for me either, so I can understand you wanting to be in denial. When you figure out it *is* that kind of party, make sure I'm one of the first to get an invitation."

Chloe slipped off her shoes before easing onto the sofa. Breakfast had been crazy and she needed to grab a private and quiet moment before preparing lunch. At times she wondered if she was growing men. There seemed to be more of them showing up for meals every day.

She smiled and inwardly admitted that she was becoming attached to each of them. They were good men, hardworking men, family men who often would talk about their wives and children and their love for them. Working for Ramsey was more than a way to keep food on the table. From the bits of conversations she'd been able to pick up, she knew they considered Ramsey a good employer, the best. He was fair and provided them with a means to provide for their families. She looked forward to seeing them every morning and didn't mind taking the time to prepare all the foods they liked.

To her surprise, and she was sure to his men as well, Ramsey had spent time with his men this morning. Of course they had teased him mercilessly before settling down to the huge meal she had prepared. And on the invitation and insistence from Ramsey, after everyone had been served, she had sat down with him at the table and had a cup of coffee when he conversed with his men. During that time she felt like a member of Ramsey's working-crew family. She felt as if she truly belonged. And she was learning more and more about Ramsey from those who knew him the best. It was great information she could use in the article she wanted to write on him.

The article she would not be writing now.

She breathed in deeply. She had come here with only one goal in mind and that was to convince Ramsey to pose on the cover of her magazine and to also obtain information to share with her readers. Considering everything, there was no way she could go through with doing that now. She had crossed over the line of what was professional, of what was right.

She did not want him to think she had gone to the extreme

and shared his bed only as a means to an end. Therefore, she needed to tell him the truth and would do so tonight when she had his complete attention, and somehow she would convince him not to send her away, but to let her work through the end of the week because his regular cook would return on Monday.

She didn't want to think about how he would possibly feel once he learned the truth. It hadn't been her intent for things to work out this way, but they had and now their time together was about to come to an end and she could feel her heart breaking. Things were beginning to get complicated. She was not only deceiving Ramsey, but she was deceiving his family as well, at least those she'd met. She needed to get out of dodge before drowning in her sea of lies.

She heard a quick tap and then the front door opened. She stood when three women walked in and she found herself under the intense gaze of three pairs of eyes the exact color of Ramsey's. She knew immediately these were his sisters.

Ramsey cursed under his breath when he pulled into his yard, recognizing the three vehicles haphazardly parked there. For his sisters to come calling at this time of the day and all at the same time meant curiosity had gotten the best of them and they were here to check things out for themselves.

He glanced in his rearview mirror, surprised Callum wasn't pulling up behind him. The man seemed to have some kind of built-in radar where Gemma was concerned. Whenever she showed up at his place, Callum homed in on her and would find just about any excuse to show up.

As he got out of his truck, the rich scent of something delectable cooking filled the air. This was Chloe's last week and he wondered how his men were going to readjust when Nellie returned. He had called and left a message on her cell phone letting her know they needed to talk before Monday. Chloe had raised the bar of expectations and although he knew Nellie was a darn good cook, she hadn't displayed a lot of that skill lately. And her attitude toward his men definitely needed improving.

But still, just the thought that this Friday would be Chloe's last day did something to him. He refused to believe what Dillon had hinted at earlier that he was developing feelings for her. Yes, he had enjoyed sleeping with her last night and intended to do so again, but he had no intention of progressing to anything remotely serious between them. He was a loner. He preferred things that way.

He heard the sound of feminine voices the moment he walked into his house. He paused and noted the chatter, the laughter, the downright friendliness in the conversations being shared. It seemed the four women were getting along, and for some reason that pleased him. Why it would, he wasn't sure.

Following the sound of the voices as well as the scent of food cooking, he headed toward the kitchen and then leaned in the doorway at the sight that greeted him. His sisters were sitting down at the table, sampling whatever was smelling so damn good, while Chloe stirred something in a big pot. If he didn't know better, by the way they were carrying on, he would have thought they had known each other for years.

"Forgive me if I'm interrupting anything," he said when it became obvious no one had noticed him.

Four pairs of eyes turned his way, but it was only one pair that he sought out. And the moment Chloe's gaze met his, he felt it, a deep stirring within the pit of his stomach, and it had more depth than just a sensual ache. He was tempted to do what he'd done this morning in front of Zane, Derringer,

Jason and Callum, which was to cross the room and take Chloe into his arms and kiss her, ignoring their audience. But there was no way in hell he could ignore the three sitting at the table who had huge smiles on their faces like he'd cut muster about something. And he couldn't help but notice they were watching him closely.

"You're not interrupting anything," Bailey said sweetly, smiling with too much saccharin on her lips to suit him. "We were just sitting here chatting with Chloe, trying to get to know her better."

He lifted a brow and almost asked why they saw fit to do something like that when Chloe would be leaving this Friday, but he refrained from doing so. "Suit yourself. If you will excuse me I have work to do."

He moved to walk toward his office wondering why he was doing the very thing he said he would no longer do where Chloe was concerned. But then he knew that putting any ideas into his sisters' heads would be dangerous. They wouldn't take it and run, they would take it and rush off in a mad dash. Besides, by retreating he was saving Chloe from being interrogated later, not that his nosy sisters hadn't probably tried pumping her for information already.

When he reached his office he eased down in the chair behind his desk wondering how long his visitors intended to stay. His men would be showing up in a few hours for lunch and he hadn't had any private time with Chloe since they'd last made love this morning. He at least wanted to kiss her the way he had wanted to do without an audience.

He picked up the folder on his desk. He would try to get some work done and hoped like hell his sisters would leave in a timely manner. Otherwise, he would be tempted to ask them to leave.

He smiled thinking doing something like that wouldn't go over well. He'd escorted them to the door before, but always in a teasing manner; however, today he would be dead serious. And he intended to do something about the locks on his back door where anyone thought they could just walk in whenever they wanted. That had never bothered him before but now it did.

He threw down the folder he'd been holding in his hands, not believing the way his thoughts were going. The only reason he was considering changing the damn lock was because on two different occasions he had been caught kissing Chloe. Because she would be leaving after Friday, did it really matter now?

He slumped back in his chair, finally admitting to himself that yes, it did matter. He didn't want things between them to end yet. He could ask Chloe to go out with him on occasion, he would take her to dinner and pursue some sort of a relationship with her. Nothing real serious, mind you. Was that what he really wanted? With lambing starting next week as well as some of his men returning to sheepherding, would he have the time? He knew at that moment he would do something he hadn't done in well over ten years and that is to make time for a woman.

He glanced up when he heard a knock on his door. His pulse leaped. Had his sisters left and Chloe had come looking for him? He stood and a frown settled on his face when Callum walked in. He dropped back down in the chair disappointed.

Ramsey didn't have to ask his friend why he was there. He knew. And the way Ramsey was feeling about his sisters at that moment, he was tempted to pay Callum a hefty fee to take Gemma off his hands. There was no hope for Megan and

Bailey. Megan wasn't dating anyone seriously since she had finally dumped that asshole of a doctor she'd gotten involved with last year. And lucky for him Bailey was more into her books than the opposite sex. She was determined to finish college in three years instead of four and then obtain a law degree. Although she could get on his last nerve at times, he was proud of her and her dedication to her studies.

"What are you doing here, Cal?" Ramsey couldn't resist the opportunity to tease his friend. Callum had given him enough grief over Chloe during the last couple of days to last a lifetime, so to Ramsey's way of thinking the ribbing was justified.

"What do you think?"

Ramsey rolled his eyes. Callum had been hanging around Zane too much lately. He was beginning to sound just like him. "You do know that one day you're going to have to take matters into your own hands, and I don't mean something as extreme as kidnapping," Ramsey said.

Callum didn't say anything, he just smiled. At any other point in time that smile would have made Ramsey uneasy, had him somewhat worried, but not today. He had his own problems to deal with and for once Callum and Gemma were the least of his concern.

His only concern was whether Chloe would be interested in continuing their relationship after Friday. And he intended to do whatever it took to make sure she wanted that as much as he did.

Nine

As soon as the last vehicle pulled out of Ramsey's yard, Chloe glanced over at him. He was leaning in the kitchen doorway staring at her. The men had arrived on time for lunch and Ramsey's sisters had stuck around to join them for the meal. Zane, Derringer and Jason had also shown up, and Callum had appeared out of the back with Ramsey, which meant he had been there for a while.

After everyone had been fed, Ramsey's sisters had been kind enough to help clear the table and help load the dishwasher. Ramsey had assisted with cleanup duty as well and in no time at all, the kitchen was spotless. If she didn't know any better Chloe would have thought Ramsey had pitched in to hurry off his sisters. Evidently they got the message and had taken Zane, Derringer and Jason right along with them. Callum had returned to the shearing plant with the men.

And now for the first time since waking up that morning,

she and Ramsey were alone. She held Ramsey's gaze as memories of last night flooded her mind. She instantly recalled his mouth on her body, how his lips had trailed over every inch of her, his tongue, hot, wet and greedy, had devoured her breasts and the area between her legs. She took a deep breath as she thought about how perfectly their bodies had fit and the sensations she'd felt with him moving inside of her.

He had been the most passionate of lovers, creative and imaginative all rolled into one, and she knew without a doubt that last night each and every one of her fantasies had been fulfilled. Whether he ever appeared on the cover of her magazine no longer mattered because she knew firsthand that Ramsey Westmoreland was indeed the most irresistible man that existed.

"Come here, Chloe."

His words, spoken in what sounded like a heated breath, floated across the room to her, touched her all over and in the very places, his hands, mouth, lips and tongue had traveled the night before.

And without hesitating, she crossed the room and walked straight into his arms. When he gripped her tightly to him, she lifted her face and stared into his eyes.

When he leaned down and captured her mouth in his, every part of her was stirred into action and she returned his kiss as hungrily as he gave it. Her chest settled against his and she knew he could feel the hardened tips of her breasts pressing into him. She could certainly feel his burgeoning erection that was cradled intimately between her thighs.

Moments later, their mouths broke apart and she felt her fingers flexed as they held on to his shoulders, otherwise she would have fallen to her knees. The sensations flowing through her heated her insides.

"I want to make love to you right here. Right now. But I can't risk any unexpected visitors," he murmured hotly against her lips. "It would greatly upset me if we got interrupted."

From the sound of his voice and his aroused expression, she knew he was serious. He wanted her just as much as she wanted him. "Then maybe we should go upstairs," she invited in a husky whisper.

From the darkening of his eyes she knew he'd heard every word she'd said. And before she could let out her next breath, he swept her off her feet and into his arms and headed toward the stairs.

Ramsey placed Chloe on the bed and stood back. He needed to look at her, study her, analyze how this woman had changed his life to the point where he was up here in his bedroom, about to make love to her, when it wasn't even three in the afternoon. There were forty million other things he could be doing around his ranch. Nearly half his herd was pregnant, lambing began next Monday and he needed to make sure all the lambing stalls were ready.

But at that moment nothing was more important to him than getting inside of Chloe, locking his body to hers, feeling her muscles clamp down on him, pulling him in and drawing every single thing out of him. Sensation was building in his erection, arousing him to the point where he wanted to tear off his clothes and hers. He wanted to mate with her. Stay inside her body and never come out.

Ramsey glanced over at her. He wanted her wet all over and easing onto the bed he reached out and pulled her to him, and began stroking his tongue along her lower lip. There was something about her mouth that enthralled him, made him want to keep kissing her, but first he wanted to taste her all over. He remembered all the things he had done to her last night, but was convinced that it had not been enough.

His hands moved to her blouse and within seconds he had pulled it over her head and tossed it aside. Then his gaze lowered to her chest and he saw how the nipples of her breasts had hardened to pebbles and were pressed against the lace material of her bra. And it was a pink bra that matched the color of the blouse he had removed earlier. He wondered if her panties would also be the same color. He'd noticed that about her last night. She had been wearing a light green lace bra and had been wearing matching lace panties. He found her color-coordinated lingerie downright sexy.

With eager fingers he undid the front closure of her bra and watched as it parted, exposing two of the most beautiful globes he'd ever seen. He had thought that very thing last night and it still held true in the bright sunlight. They were perfect for his hands and incredibly delicious to his mouth.

Removing the bra completely he leaned forward and captured a hard nipple between his lips and then his tongue went to work, reacquainting his taste buds with the flavor he had enjoyed last night while holding her breast firmly in his hand.

He heard her soft moans as he feasted on one breast and then another, taking his time while his tongue so effortlessly devoured her. It felt hot, inflamed as it went about licking her hungrily, sucking the tip greedily. Never before had he gotten such pleasure from such an assault on a woman's breasts.

He finally lifted his head and pulled back as a slow smile touched his lips. Without saying anything he gently eased her back while his hands went to her skirt and he gently pulled the denim material down her hips, thighs and legs, leaving her in those leggings. A pretty pink pair.

He studied the footless tights and although he much preferred seeing her legs bare as they had been last night, there was something about all those colorful leggings she wore that definitely made a statement. But at that moment he was going to enjoy peeling the damn things off her.

"You do know I really don't like these things," he said as he reached for the waistband.

She quirked a brow at him. "Why?"

He smiled and said simply. "They hide your legs."

Chloe smiled. "Leggings are part of the latest fashion trend. And they don't hide my legs, Ramsey, they accent them. Usually my dresses or skirts are rather short. Leggings work well with my outfits and with the flat shoes I normally wear it makes the perfect casual outfit."

Ramsey nodded, not believing he was actually discussing a woman's attire.

"Would you prefer I not wear leggings while I'm around your men, Ramsey?"

His answer was quick in coming. "No."

"Okay, then, rancher. You can't have it both ways."

He sort of disagreed with that. "In private I'm taking them off you because I love looking at your legs."

"Suit yourself."

And he intended to, he thought. And then his throat tightened, not allowing another word to slip through when he inched the leggings past her hips to uncover a very skimpy, very sexy pink thong.

Once he had peeled the leggings completely off her, his attention went back to that very hot-looking thong, dying to reveal what it covered and deciding not to wait.

Adjusting his body he slouched down on the bed between her open legs and lifted them on his shoulders. And just like last night, the feel of those bare legs on his shoulders, smooth and silky, rubbing against his skin made the lower part of him throb with an intensity that sent shudders through his body. And it wasn't helping matters that he was drowning in her scent. Being this intimately close to her hot mound made him crave her taste even more.

As soon as he felt he was in the right position, he leaned in and flicked his tongue across her crotch, dampening her thong in the process but getting a taste of what was behind it. She moaned and the sound went straight to his erection and made it surge.

"What are you doing to me?" she asked, in a voice that seemed strained, breathless, panting.

"What does it feel like?" He flicked his tongue across her again, wanting her to feel the strength behind it. "But if what I'm doing is bothering you, I can always stop," he said and grinned at her.

"No," she said quickly. "Please don't stop."

He glanced up at her and his response was just as quick. "I won't." The look he saw in her face, blatant need and transparent pleasure, fueled his hunger and he pulled back slightly, lifted her hips to remove the thong from her body.

He had gotten his first taste of her in this very feminine hot spot last night and had been craving more of her ever since. He hadn't known the extent of his sexual desire until he'd made love to her. When he recalled all the orgasms they had shared last night, his desperation in wanting her again was warranted.

Tossing the skimpy undergarment aside, he eased back in place between her thighs and rubbed his chin against her naked skin, liking the feel of her and the look of her Brazilian wax. Not able to hold back any longer, he began licking at her, taking his tongue and outlining her feminine mound wanting her to feel the urgency of his desire.

"Ramsey," she called out his name in a whispered tone as she tightened the legs around his shoulder.

"Yes, baby?" he asked in a deep tone.

"I—I like that."

A shiver swept through him. "I like it, too." And then he showed her just how much when he parted her feminine folds and let his tongue go to work. Her taste stirred a yearning in him that could only be appeased this particular way and by doing this precise thing. And the sound of her moans, her whimpers, the tightening of her legs around his shoulders, and the sweet liquor her body was producing, sent what seemed like an unquenchable greed through him.

He knew it was only a matter of time before she came and when that thought raced through him the pressure of his tongue inside of her increased, lapping her up like his very life depended on it. And when he felt Chloe's body jerk beneath his mouth he held on tight, knowing her spasms would soon become his.

They did. And with as much pleasure as his mental state could take, he went for the gusto, using his tongue to push her even more so over the edge while keeping his mouth locked tight to her.

Chloe was convinced her mind was splintering under the intensity of the explosion that ripped through her. She breathed in sharply and felt the lower half of her body actually being lifted off the bed, but Ramsey was there, holding on tight to her, gripping her hips, keeping her bolted to his mouth.

His tongue was assaulting her core as he continued to lap her up. She screamed out his name as spasms, as vicious as they could get, tore into her, spinning her senses out of control and into a turmoil or passion.

It was only when the last tremble passed through her that he released her and pulled back. There was nothing she could do but slump back on the bed. She felt weaker than water. She watched through partially closed lashes as he moved from the bed to remove his clothes.

She could only lay there, trying to get her breathing back to normal as she watched him lean over to take off his boots. He then straightened to unbutton his shirt and then eased it off his muscular shoulders and tossed it aside. Sliding the brass buckle belt through the loops, he lowered his zipper before pushing the jeans down his legs.

Even while lying there, with barely enough energy to breathe, Chloe watched as Ramsey removed every stitch of clothing and then he stood, fully naked and all male. Her eyes latched on his erection, big and powerful, and upon seeing it, fiery sensations swept through her, giving her renewed energy while stirring desire within her all over again.

When he reached into the nightstand to retrieve a condom packet and tore it open with his teeth, before proceeding to roll it over his swollen shaft, she felt what amounted to fire raging through her veins. She exhaled a deep breath when he came back to the bed and with gentle hands he reached out and eased her legs apart.

Moments later, in position between them, he leaned down and captured her lips in a kiss so painstakingly tender that it almost brought tears to her eyes and made her fall in love with him that much more. When he tore his lips from her to pull back, he tilted her hips up to him before surging deep within her. The pleasure she felt with his entry sent a moan from deep within her throat. And then the mating of their bodies began as he eased in and out of her, giving her the pleasure her body was aching for.

"Look at me, baby. Feel me," Ramsey said as his fingertips caressed her chin.

She did feel him. He was as deep as he could get and his need was raging just as out of control as hers. Then he picked up the tempo and she clung to him, determined to meet him on every level. Especially this one.

And when he called out her name in a guttural growl she knew that here, in bed, making love, the two of them were in the same sensual vibe. And when she cried out her pleasure, felt her body explode yet again, and knew he was following her over the edge, she could have sworn at that moment she actually felt his hot release shooting inside of her, all the way to the womb. But she knew that wasn't possible. She had watched him put on a condom. It was nothing more than her imagination at work, and when he continued to drive hard within her she knew the night was just beginning.

A long time later Chloe lay in Ramsey's arms in the position she'd discovered he liked the best: spoon style. Her backside was cushioned by his front and his muscular leg was thrown over hers. Her head was resting back on his chest and his arm was thrown over her middle.

She felt satiated, relaxed, secured. After their last lovemaking session, Ramsey had eased out of her and had gone into the bathroom to discard the condom and to put on another. He liked being ready and chances were today would not be any different than last night when they had made love, rested and made love again all through the night. However, at some point they needed to prepare something for dinner to keep up their strength.

They enjoyed each other and she couldn't see them not

making love several more times before they finally drifted off to sleep. The thought that he desired her as much as she desired him made her heart thump rapidly in her chest.

She pulled in a deep breath knowing she had to level with him. No matter how he handled things she needed to tell him the truth. She would let him know she no longer wanted him to pose for the cover, nor did she want to do an article on him.

Knowing it was best to just get it over with, she turned into his arms. She could tell the move surprised him and deciding to just tell him and not waste any time, she took a quick breath and said, "Ramsey, there's something I need to tell you."

Ramsey quickly placed a finger to Chloe's lips. Knowing his sisters and how desperate they were for him to become involved with a woman, they had probably gone overboard, shaken her up by tossing her some ideas she wasn't quite ready to catch. So she was about to bail out. Let him know that for her things weren't quite that serious. He understood, but he wasn't ready to hear her acknowledge that yet.

At the end of the week, right before she left for good, then they would talk. He would tell her of his desire to see her again when her work here ended. He wanted to take her out, make love to her, he wanted for them to continue what they had started here. He recalled what he'd said to Dillon earlier that day and knew that he *did* want it to be that kind of a party.

"Let's not get into a serious discussion about anything. Not now. We can discuss any serious topics on your last day. I need to continue to have the peace I've found with you, Chloe. Could you hold your thoughts for a while and give me that?"

She slowly nodded. "Yes, I can give you that."

"And," he continued by saying, "with shearing wrapping

up this week, the sheep that's not pregnant will be taken to pasture and—"

"You have a lot of sheep pregnant?"

He smiled. "Yes, almost half my herd."

He saw the look of surprise on her face. "How did that many sheep get pregnant at the same time?"

"It's timed that way. The female sheep, the ewes, are put out with the rams during mating season and five months later they deliver during what is call lambing. That's when the lamb is born. Luckily ewes won't deliver the same day, but typically they will all deliver within a two-week period of each other."

"Wow!"

He chuckled. In a way he was pleased with Chloe's interest in his ranch. "The rams and the wethers are—"

"Wethers?"

"Yes, castrated male sheep," he explained. "While the pregnant ewes are lambing, the rams and wethers and the ewes that aren't pregnant are taken to pasture by the sheepherders. And that is where most of them will be for the next few months out on the pasture grazing."

An idea popped into his head. "One of my men, Pete Overton, won't be able to begin sheepherding until Sunday morning, so I'm going to drive his herd out to pasture early Saturday morning and get things all set up for him. Will you come with me? We'll be back here before noon Sunday."

Chloe smiled up at Ramsey. She had wanted to come clean and tell him the truth, but he preferred they hold off and not discuss anything serious until her last day. That was fine with her because she knew that once she told him the truth he would probably be upset with her.

She leaned up and wrapped her arms around his neck. "Yes, I'd love to go with you."

Ten

Over the next few days Chloe accepted the realization that she was falling in love with Ramsey. They would share a bed each night and get up before daybreak every morning and together they would prepare breakfast for the men.

It was during those times that he would share more information about his life as a sheepherder and had begun telling her about members of his family. Five of his siblings had been under sixteen when his parents had gotten killed— Megan, Gemma, the twins by the name of Adrian and Aiden, and his sister Bailey. Zane had been a senior in high school, ready to go off to college and Derringer had been about to enter his senior year of high school. His cousin Dillon had been placed in a similar situation with four siblings under sixteen.

From what Ramsey told her, Adrian and Aiden were now in their last year of college at Harvard, as was their cousin

Stern. Another cousin by the name of Canyon was in medical school at Howard University in D.C. Brisbane was in the Navy. Micah, who was Zane's counterpart in age, was a graduate from Harvard Medical School and was an epidemiologist with the federal government.

Just listening to Ramsey share information with her about his family's turbulent years and the struggle that he and Dillon had had to endure to keep their families together, she had to admire the two men. Although she had yet to meet Dillon, she had met another one of his brothers, Riley, and found him to be just as handsome as the others.

And Ramsey had shared more information about sheepherding with her. One afternoon they had walked around his ranch. He had taken her to where the lambing stalls were and explained how next week more than a thousand of his ewes would be delivering. She had found the whole process fascinating. He had also given her a tour of the shearing plant and she was able to watch the men at work. She'd seen the dogs at work, too, and Ramsey had explained how important the sheepdogs were in managing and protecting the herds. You could definitely see that running a sheep ranch required maintaining a tight schedule and sticking to it.

Hanging the last pot back on the rack, she turned when she heard the back door open and smiled when Ramsey walked in. Closing the door behind him, and without missing a step, he crossed the kitchen floor and pulled her into his arms and kissed her.

Chloe returned the kiss, for the moment refusing to acknowledge that she was making it harder and harder to leave after this weekend, to walk away and not to look back. The thought of doing so caused her heart to ache, but that's what she would be doing. She decided she didn't want to think beyond it, so she tightened her arms around him as he deepened his kiss. His mouth slanted against hers and she could feel her knees weaken.

Moments later he broke off the kiss and pulled back slightly and whispered against her moist lips. "Why do you always taste so sweet?"

His words further eroded her sensibility. He sounded so serious like there was truly an answer for his question. There wasn't one, so she shook her head, tilted it up and smiled at him. "For the same reason you always taste so delicious."

And to show him just what she meant, she took the tip of her tongue and licked a corner of his mouth. The instant she did, his long eyelashes swept upward to reveal the depths of his darkened gaze, and she could just imagine what he was thinking now.

"Doing something like that can get you into trouble," he warned, as his arms tightened around her waist, drawing her even closer into the fit of his muscular form.

She smiled. "So you say."

"So I can prove." He took a step away from her. "But not now. First, I need to let you know that we've been invited to dinner."

She lifted a brow. "Dinner?"

"Yes, my cousin Dillon and his wife Pamela want to meet you."

Panic settled into Chloe's bones. She didn't want to pull any more of Ramsey's family members into her web of deceit. She liked all of the ones she'd met so far and from what she'd heard about the oldest Denver Westmoreland, Dillon, there was no doubt in her mind that she would like him as well.

"Why do they want to meet me?" she asked, not sure she was ready to meet the man Ramsey was so close to.

"They've heard a lot of nice things about you and want to meet you for themselves."

She didn't know what to say to that. She had heard a lot of nice things about them as well. "I bet it was Jason who told them how I could fix his eggs just the way he likes them," she said in a teasing voice, trying to make light of what Ramsey had said.

Ramsey chuckled. "Might be. Or it could have been one of my brothers or sisters. You've made quite an impression on them."

Chloe glanced down to study the floor. At any other time knowing she had impressed the family of the man she loved would have been a feather in her cap. But not now. When they found out the truth it won't just be Ramsey who'd think she'd deceived them. Lucia had been right. Chloe had been around them long enough to know the Westmorelands stuck together and if you were to hurt one, then you hurt them all.

"So, will you go to dinner with me at Dillon and Pamela's?"

A part of her wanted to come up with an excuse not to go. She should claim a headache or something, but she could not do that. Although she deserved nothing, she wanted it all. She wanted to get to know more about the man she had fallen in love with. As well as to get to know those he loved and those who loved him.

She pulled in a deep breath and then said, "Yes, I'll go to dinner with you."

Ramsey could not remember the last time he'd brought a woman to a family function. Even with the annual charity ball they sponsored each year for the Westmoreland Foundation that had been established to aid various community causes, he usually went solo. For him it had been better that way and because there had been enough eager-beaver Westmorelands who enjoyed being the center on attention with beautiful women on their arms, he was left alone.

He couldn't even recall bringing Danielle to dinner when they'd dated. He never had to bother because his mother had liked Danielle enough to invite her to dinner whenever she saw her at church most Sundays. He knew the main reason he had dated Danielle as long as he had was because his family had liked her. And then because she'd hung around waiting for him to finish college, he had felt marrying her was the least he could do.

The truth of the matter was that she hadn't been idle while she'd waited. At some point she had met someone, slept with the person and had gotten pregnant. The sad thing about it was that the man never married her and she ended up being a single mom.

He glanced around the room thinking that this was not supposed to be a family function. Dillon and Pamela had invited him and Chloe to dinner and they had accepted. He had expected to see Pamela's three younger sisters because this was spring break back in Gamble. But he hadn't expected to see his three sisters who were smiling sweetly at him at every turn. Nor had he expected to see Zane, Derringer and Jason. He saw them enough around his place for breakfast and lunch. Callum was not a surprise because the man took advantage of every opportunity to hang around Gemma. Riley wasn't a surprise either because he was known to drop in whenever and wherever there was a free meal.

"You might have disappointed me for not doing that magazine cover, but you've more than made up for it with Chloe, Ram. I like her," Bailey said.

Ramsey turned and met his baby sister's gaze. "And just

what do you like about her?" he asked, curious to hear what she had to say.

"She fits you."

Because he'd been expecting a long, drawn out discourse, he was surprised by those three words. This was definitely a night for surprises, but then he thought he would not let Bailey get off that easily. "She fits me in what way?"

Bailey shrugged. "She's pretty. You're handsome. She can cook. You can't. She's an extrovert. You're an introvert." She lifted her brow. "Need I go on?"

"No."

"Because we all know you have a tendency to stretch things out, Ram. If you are interested in her, you probably want to step up your game a notch."

Now it was his time to raise a brow. "What makes you think I'm interested in her?" he asked, glancing across the room to where Chloe sat talking to Pamela. The two women were getting along like they were old friends.

"She's here isn't she? That in itself says a lot." And without saying anything else, Bailey strolled off.

He was tempted to follow Bailey and tell her that no, nothing said it all. They were seeing things that weren't there. Seeing what they wanted to see. But when he glanced back over at Chloe, he was beginning to wonder if perhaps everything that Bailey had said just now made sense. If so, that was real scary only because it was Bailey and she never thought logically.

Not for the first time tonight Chloe quickly glanced over at Ramsey before turning her full attention back to the conversation going on around her. The topic of conversation had shifted from just how good the First Lady had looked at a nationally televised event last evening to what was happening overseas.

More than once he had caught her gaze and the smile he'd sent her way was enough to send heat escalating through every part of her body. And memories of his touch would wash over her, make her wish they were someplace else. Someplace private.

"So you're an only child, Chloe?"

Chloe glanced up at Gemma and smiled. The Westmorelands had been asking her questions about herself. Getting to know her. She had been wording her answers so they wouldn't be outright lies. "Yes, I'm an only child but not for long. My father is getting married in a few months and the person he's marrying has a son and daughter."

"And you don't have a problem with that?" Bailey asked.

Chloe chuckled. "Not at all. Dad's been single long enough. My mother died when I was two, so it's about time he tied the knot again."

The conversation shifted to Megan as she told them how her day went as an anesthesiologist. Chloe glanced back across the room at Ramsey. He was talking to Dillon. There was no mistaking the two men were related. Dillon Westmoreland was also a good-looking man.

Ramsey caught her eye and like before, the look he gave her made her heart thump erratically in her chest. And as she continued to look at him she could actually feel his heat, reaching out across the perimeters of the room and actually touch her. And then he whispered something to Dillon before walking across the room toward her.

When he reached her side he tucked her hand in his, something that wasn't missed by his sisters. "Thanks, Pamela, for a lovely dinner. It's time Chloe and I left."

Chloe glanced up at him, not surprised by what he said. It was either leave so they could go somewhere private or put on a real show for his family.

Pamela glanced at her watch. "It's early yet. Are you sure you have to go?"

Ramsey smiled. "Yes, trust us, we do."

Later that night Ramsey was wide awake as he watched Chloe sleep. They had barely made it through the front door before they began stripping out of their clothes. They hadn't thought about making it up the stairs to the bedroom; instead they had been satisfied just to get to the sofa. By the time he had slid his body into hers, all the restraints he'd held in place over the past twelve hours came crashing down.

He had made love to her with an intensity that had even overwhelmed him. She had writhed beneath him, filled with the same turbulent need as she strained against him, meeting his strokes, his single-minded thrusts as if her very life depended on it.

She had dug her nails into his shoulders and on one or two occasions, had actually bit him. He had growled and then had increased the pace as his control and hers had continued to get shot to hell. He gave it to her hard, and at her encouragement, even harder. She had transformed into a wildcat, a woman who knew the degree of pleasure she'd wanted to experience. A woman who intended for him to give her just what she needed.

And he had. The more she'd wanted, the more he'd given. And by the time their world exploded into one hell of a combined orgasm, he was barely holding on the edge of sanity. He had known the moment pleasure had ripped his soul apart that this was not just a normal lovemaking session between two consenting adults. It was a hell of a lot more than that.

The word *normal* didn't even come close. There had been nothing ordinary about their joining. It had been the most atypical thing he'd ever experienced.

And now he knew why.

For the first time in his life he wanted to have a serious relationship with a woman. And he now knew more than ever that what he felt for Chloe wasn't just a sexual thing. Tomorrow was officially her last day at the ranch, although she had agreed to spend Friday and Saturday night with him on the range sheepherding.

He could tell from the murmurs he'd been hearing over the past couple of days from his men that she would be missed, and it wasn't just about the meals she had prepared for them. It was about the woman they had come to know. A woman who took joy in making their nourishment.

Yet she had remained professional while developing friendships with them. They looked forward to seeing her in the morning and again at noon. She not only talked to them, but she also listened. On occasion, he knew she also offered advice to a couple of the men when they'd inquired as to what to purchase their wives for birthday and anniversary gifts.

They would miss her, but none of them would miss her more than he would. In just two short weeks she had touched him, given him a bone-deep feeling of total and complete satisfaction, one he could not have explained until now.

He leaned over and brushed a kiss across her brow. Last week he could barely make sense of what was happening to him, but now he knew and accepted his fate. He loved this woman. He really loved her.

And he wanted to keep her.

He knew that might be easier said than done. She might not want to have a relationship with him, one with the potential of going somewhere. She might like her life like it was now—not seriously involved with anyone. That Daren guy had probably left a bad taste in her mouth. In that case, he would do whatever he needed to do to make her change her attitude about a serious affair.

Unfortunately he did not have Callum's patience. Starting now he would rev up his campaign to win her over, prevail in getting her love. At least his situation didn't appear to be as hopeless as Dillon's had been when he'd met Pamela. At the time she was engaged to marry someone else. But with his encouragement Dillon hadn't let that stop him.

Now was time to take some of the same advice he'd dished out to Dillon. He knew what he wanted and there was no excuse in his not getting it. He had a goal. By this time next year Chloe Burton would have a permanent place in his bed as his wife.

"Are you okay, Chloe?"

Chloe glanced over at Ramsey. No, she wasn't okay. Saying goodbye to his men had been the hardest thing she'd ever had to do. And she had fought back tears when they'd given her a going-away gift.

"Yes, I'm okay," she said, knowing she really wasn't. Ramsey had helped her to clean up the kitchen after lunch and then she had thrown a couple of items into an overnight bag. When she had stepped outside it was to find a huge RV parked in his yard. He had explained that the modern-day sheepherder believed in living out on the range with all the conveniences of home. Granted most didn't have anything this large and extravagant. The majority of them did have campers that they pulled behind their trucks and would set up residence without having to sacrifice doing without satellite television, indoor bathroom and kitchen and dining facilities.

The luxury coach Ramsey was driving was his own personal beauty and as Chloe glanced around she was impressed with just how nice it was, and how much an expert driver he was behind the wheel. This was definitely a luxury coach worth owning. It was a home away from home on wheels. His men had already taken the sheep up in the high country, a portion of Ramsey's land that connected to Dillon's. Chloe hadn't been aware of how much property the Westmorelands owned until now.

"The men are going to miss you."

She smiled. "And I'm going to miss them."

"And I'm going to miss you as well, Chloe."

Chloe thought about the words Ramsey had just spoken as she watched him kill the engine of the RV. He glanced over at her and the pull that was always there between them was tugging at her today in the worst possible way. "And I'm going to miss you, too, Ramsey."

He leaned over and she was there, meeting him halfway over the vehicle's console. And when their mouths connected she thought that nothing could get any better than this.

He pulled back, but not before taking his tongue to swipe across her lower lip. "Come on, let's get out so I can show you the rest of the property while there's still daylight."

Moments later, holding hands they walked near the area where the sheep were grazing. One of Ramsey's men, Pete Overton, smiled when they approached. "Now that you're here boss, I'll just skedaddle so I'll be on time for the party." Pete's oldest son would be graduating from the university tomorrow and his wife had planned a party in his honor. Ramsey had volunteered to tend to the sheep until Pete came back to relieve him Sunday morning.

"Sure, Pete, and give Pete Jr. my congratulations and best wishes. I know that you and Jayne are proud of him."

Pete beamed proudly. "Thanks, Ram." He then glanced at Chloe and his smile got even wider. "The guys and I meant what we said earlier today, Miss Chloe. You're going to be missed. Nobody makes homemade biscuits quite like you do."

Chloe returned his smile. "Thanks, Pete." They then turned and watched Pete get in his truck and leave.

"Pete is a person who doesn't take to people easily, but it's plain to see that he likes you," Ramsey said, wrapping his arms tightly around Chloe's waist.

She leaned into him. "I know," she murmured, resting her head back against Ramsey's chest. "I like him, too. I like all the men who work for you."

Ramsey introduced her to the four dogs that would be manning the herd and told her the animals made a sheepherder's job relatively simple. The dogs were the ones who looked after the flock, making sure none of the sheep wandered off and alerted the sheepherder to any mishaps.

After Ramsey gave her a tour of the area where the sheep would be grazing for the next few months, they returned to the travel coach and ate the sandwiches Ramsey had purchased from a deli in town.

Then when it got dark he took out folding chairs so they could sit outside under the stars. They ended up doing a lot more than just sitting under the stars. Ramsey selected a nice spot to spread a huge blanket on the ground where they made love, under the beauty of a Colorado sky. Later when the night turned chilly, they went inside the coach and after taking a shower they tumbled in bed to make love all over again.

The next morning after a breakfast they had prepared

together, they walked the area checking on the sheep. After lunch they curled up in each other's arms on the sofa and watched several video movies. Chloe could tell that neither she nor Ramsey wanted anything to intrude on their idyllic weekend.

Ramsey told her about how he'd grieved after the deaths of his parents and his beloved aunt and uncle. He explained how he'd had to put aside his grief to care for his siblings.

She was touched that he'd shared details about that heartbreaking moment in his life. She was tempted to share things with him as well. She wanted to tell him that although she was too young to remember much about her mother, what she had recalled while growing up was the sadness that always appeared in her father's eyes on her mother's birthday, their anniversary day and during the holidays. That was one of the reasons she was glad for the happiness in her father's life now. But there was no way she could tell Ramsey that without telling him everything and he'd made it known he wasn't ready for any hard-and-heavy discussions between them.

Later that night they showered again together. The moment he pulled her inside the shower with him and water began spraying down on their naked bodies, Ramsey turned her into his arms and kissed her, while pinning her back against the wall.

He reached up and turned off the water and then getting down on his knees, he spread open her thighs to get the taste he always seemed to want and was intent on getting whenever he could.

The sensations he could evoke with his tongue inside of her had Chloe moaning and it took all she could not to scream out loud. Ramsey had introduced her to lovemaking in its richest form; positions that were so erotic her knees weakened at the thought of some of them.

She did scream when his tongue delved deeper into her and she gripped tight to his shoulder. And just when she thought she couldn't take any more, he eased up, lifted her to wrap her legs around his waist and then he plunged into her.

With whipcord speed he began thrusting inside of her as another scream from her filled the shower stall. She then heard herself begging and pleading for more, for him not to stop and to do it harder. Those were words she never thought she would utter, which proved just how over the edge she was. Just how Ramsey's lovemaking had torn up her mind.

Her legs tightened around his waist even more, locked him inside of her as much as possible. He threw his head back and let out a curling snarl that sounded like pain, but the look of his face showed it was definitely one of pleasure.

His features distorted in sexual gratification were a mirror of what she was feeling. And when she felt him explode inside of her, she felt her world get rocked as he continued to pump inside of her as impassioned heat rushed all through her body. And then he leaned closer to her and captured her mouth in his.

His kiss snatched her breath and, combined with the shudders ripping through her, was almost too much. His kiss was hungrier than before, just as intense. And when he finally released her mouth, she slumped against his wet chest. Regaining strength to lift her head, she met his intense gaze and it took everything within her to hold back from telling him that she had fallen in love with him.

Pete returned to relieve Ramsey early Sunday morning. Ramsey couldn't wait to get back to the ranch so that he and Chloe could have a serious talk. If he had any doubts in his mind that he loved her, then this weekend only confirmed it. He hoped he would be able to put into words how he felt and why he wanted them to continue what they'd started.

He glanced over at her. She'd gotten quiet on him and he would allow her this private time. He'd come close twice this weekend of telling her how much he loved her. But he'd held back, not wanting to screw things up.

He drew in a deep breath when they pulled into his yard. Butterflies were going off in his stomach. He'd never been nervous around a woman before. Hell, he'd practically raised three of them. But this was different. It wasn't every day that a man poured out his heart the way he planned to do. But he had to be careful how he did it. He didn't want to run the risk of scaring her off.

"Will you be talking to Nellie before she returns tomorrow, Ramsey?"

Her question broke the silence that surrounded them in the RV. He turned off the engine and leaned back in his seat. "Yes. She's supposed to call today."

"Good."

Ramsey couldn't help but smile. He found it amusing how loyal she was to his men. He parked the RV on the side of the barn and when they got out they walked to the house holding hands. For him it seemed such a natural thing to do.

Ramsey opened the door and once inside Chloe said, "How would you like a cup of coffee?"

"I'd love one. Thanks."

At that moment the phone rang. "That's probably Nellie calling. I told her I'd return this morning around eleven."

Chloe nodded as she headed for the kitchen.

"Hello?"

"Mr. Westmoreland?"

Ramsey didn't recognize the feminine voice. "Yes?"

"This is Marie Dodson of the CDS Employment Agency and I regret we were unable to serve your needs before. However, if you're still in need of a ranch cook, I have someone who might work out for you, and she's—"

"Whoa," Ramsey said, cutting in, confused by what the woman was saying. "You did serve my needs. The woman you sent to us two weeks ago worked out perfectly and—"

"There must be some mistake. We didn't send a woman to work for you."

Now Ramsey was *really* confused. "Sure you did. Chloe Burton."

There was a slight pause and then, "There's no Chloe Burton working for us. The woman we had planned to send you was Constance Kennard. Because of a mix-up, she was sent to another job by mistake. I called myself that Monday morning around nine-thirty to inform you of what happened but was told you weren't available. The woman who answered your phone said she would make sure that you got the message about what happened."

A knot tightened in Ramsey's stomach and a frown settled between his brows. What Marie Dodson was saying didn't make sense. Chloe had shown up that morning. She'd been late but she had shown up. And there was no doubt in his mind that Chloe could cook. Every single man in his employ could attest to that. But if what Ms. Dodson was saying was true then…"

"Mr. Westmoreland?"

Ramsey pulled in a deep breath. "I'm going to have to call you back Ms. Dodson."

"Oh? Well, okay."

No sooner had Ramsey hung up the phone, Chloe walked

in with two coffee cups in her hands. Ramsey stopped her in her tracks when he asked in a fierce and angry voice. "Who the hell are you?"

Eleven

Chloe was knocked speechless by Ramsey's question. Pulling in a deep breath she thought it best to place the cups of coffee on the table before spilling them all over herself. Her hands were shaking because she had an idea why he'd asked what he had.

She exhaled a nervous breath before she spoke. "That's a crazy question, Ramsey. You know who I am. I'm Chloe Burton."

"Are you?"

"Yes."

He crossed his arms over his chest. "And you work for CDS Employment Agency?"

"No."

He lifted a brow. "No?"

She nodded. "No. I don't work for CDS."

He frowned. "Well, who do you work for then? I didn't contact any other employment agency for a cook."

"I work for myself."

She could tell her answer surprised him. "Yourself?"

"Yes, and while I'm at it, I might as well tell you that I'm not really a cook. I enjoy cooking but normally do so for pleasure."

Ramsey didn't say anything for a long time, he just stared at her with an intense look in his eyes. He was angry to a degree that she had never seen before in him. Even when they'd been at odds with each other during that first week, he hadn't been this angry.

"I'm going to ask you one more time," he said through gritted teeth. "Who are you? If the employment agency didn't send you and you're not a bona fide ranch cook, then who are you and why did you pretend to be Nellie's replacement?"

Her hands nervously clenched into fists at her side. Now she wished that she had been more insistent when she'd wanted to tell him the truth a week ago. There was no doubt in her mind that now he would think the worst of her.

She stared at him, saw the hard, cold look in his eyes and knew it was too late. She cleared her throat. "I saw you last month in downtown Denver, going into a feed store. I thought then that you would be perfect."

"Perfect for what?" he almost asked in a snarl.

She swallowed deeply. "To be on the cover of *Simply Irresistible* magazine."

She watched the expression on his face as the implications of what she'd said became clear. "Do you mean to tell me that you work for that magazine?"

She shook her head. "Not exactly."

His eyes narrowed. "Then what exactly?"

She nibbled on her bottom lip. "I don't work there exactly. I own the magazine."

The next thing Chloe thought was that if looks could kill, she would definitely be dead...but not before getting sheared first. She watched Ramsey's lips tighten, his jaw clench and the eyes that glared at her appeared to be dark orbs. "And just what were you doing here that morning?"

"I had come to talk to you about being featured in my magazine," she answered.

"Why?" he said in a tone so sharp it almost made her flinch. "I'd told the person who called I wasn't interested."

"I know, but I wanted to meet with you personally. Try to persuade you to change your mind."

He shook his head. "So instead you decided to pretend to be my cook and sleep with me?"

She did flinch at that. "No. That's not true. I tried to tell you the reason I was here, but you were in a hurry to leave that morning and you left me here with your front door wide open."

"Because I assumed you were the cook," he snapped.

"I never told you I was the cook, Ramsey. And you assumed wrong. Once I walked inside your house, the phone rang. It was the lady from the employment agency who said that the cook you were expecting wouldn't be coming. I could have left you in a hot mess, especially after you indicated you would have twenty hungry men to feed come lunchtime. But I decided to help you out."

"Why? So I could feel I owed you something and do that damn cover?"

"Initially, yes. I'd even planned to squeeze an interview out of you as well."

She could tell her answer, as honest as it could get, only

made him angrier. She saw it in his features to such a point where she actually felt her heart in her throat. "But like I said, that was at first, Ramsey. Once I got to know you—"

"Spare me. Lady, you have some nerve. Pretending to be someone else and—"

"And what? Helped you out for two weeks? I tried to tell you the truth a few days ago, but you wouldn't listen. You said we would put off any serious talk until today. So you can't hold that against me."

Ramsey snorted at that and the scowl on his face deepened. "I can hold it against you and I do. You should never have been here under false pretenses in the first place. As far as having a cook, I would have worked something out. You didn't need to do me any favors. And regardless of what you did for me, I still would not have posed on the cover of that magazine, so your plan wouldn't work."

"Once I got to know you, Ramsey, the cover didn't matter anymore," she implored, thinking she had never met a more bull-headed man.

"And you expect me to believe that?" he asked in an angry tone.

"Yes."

"Is there anything else you've failed to tell me?"

She shrugged. "My father is a senator from Florida. Senator Jamison Burton. My mother died when I was two and my father raised me by himself. My home is in Florida."

Ramsey stared at her, not believing what little he'd known about her.

"And the reason I could not deceive you any longer, the reason I wanted to tell you the truth that day after we'd made love was because I knew I was falling in love with you."

He stared at her for a long moment. "If being dishonest is

your idea of falling in love, Chloe, then you need to keep your love to yourself because I don't want any part of it."

He breathed in deeply and grabbed his Stetson off the rack. "I'm leaving and I want you packed up and out of here by the time I get back."

And then he walked out the door, slamming it shut behind him.

Ramsey's hands tightened on the steering wheel of his truck as he drew in a deep breath, not believing what had just taken place. What he had just walked away from. And just to think he'd intended to pour his heart out to Chloe, tell her how much he loved her, and all it had been for her was nothing more than a sinister plan to get him to pose on the cover of that damn magazine.

A part of him felt torn up inside, absolutely wrecked. Anger, the likes he'd never known before, was consuming him. He was driving with no particular destination in mind. It was Sunday, and most of his family had gone to church. Dillon and Pamela had left for the airport that morning to return to Gamble, and Callum and Zane had driven to see a rodeo in Oklahoma. Maybe it was for the best because he sure as hell didn't feel like socializing with anyone right now.

He pulled over to the side of the road and hit his fist against the steering wheel. How could he have been so stupid to let his guard down? Why was he always the last to know anything about a woman's trickery? It hadn't been any different with Danielle. Although he'd been relieved she'd ended the wedding, the fact still remained that she had made a fool of him.

He pulled back into the road. He'd meant what he said. Chloe had better be gone by the time he got back. And he hoped like hell that he never saw her again.

* * *

"Here, drink this," Lucia said, handing Chloe a cup of herbal tea. "It will help your headache."

Chloe glanced up at her friend, not wanting to tell her it wasn't her head that was hurting as much as her heart. "Thanks," she said, accepting the cup of hot tea.

"And now you need to go take a shower and get into bed."

Chloe rolled her eyes. "Lou, it's the middle of the day."

"Yes, but a nap might make you feel better."

Chloe shrugged. "I doubt it." She knew nothing would make her feel better unless Ramsey was to walk through that door and tell her that he believed her, that he knew she truly did love him, and that even though she had planned on making him indebted to her initially, she had discarded that plan once she'd fallen in love with him.

An hour later Chloe still sat curled up on Lucia's sofa. Lucia had finally left to go have Sunday dinner with her parents. Chloe felt she needed this time alone to go back over and over in her mind what happened earlier that day at Ramsey's house, and everything else that had transpired from the moment she'd driven onto his property over two weeks ago.

She thought of the angry words he had spoken to her before he'd left his home, ordering her to pack up and leave before he got back. A part of her had wanted to rebel and be there when he returned to have it out with him. But then there was nothing she could say that she hadn't already said.

And he hadn't believed her.

It had been a teary ride from Ramsey's ranch all the way to Lucia's home, and now she knew she couldn't remain in Denver. It was clear as the nose on her face that there wa nothing here for her anymore. But a part of her refused to run.

Chances were her and Ramsey's paths would not cross anytime soon, so that would give her the time she needed to recover from a broken heart.

His men were watching him and Ramsey was well aware that they'd been watching him off and on for the past couple of weeks. Today he would do something he usually didn't do. Ignore them.

And for good reason. They wanted something he could not deliver. They wanted Chloe back. Nellie had returned and although he'd had a talk with her before allowing her back in his kitchen, after one good week she was sliding back into her old ways. The men, like him, were comparing what they had now with what they'd had for two weeks.

A part of Ramsey wanted to shout at them, to tell them that although Chloe's cooking skills were superb, she was not a cook. She had done it for fun. It had been all a part of her deliberate scheme to get him indebted to her.

His cell phone rang and he welcomed the excuse to leave the table and answer it in private. He had stepped into the living room when he spoke into his cell after checking the Caller ID. "Yes, Dillon?"

"I was asked to call and talk to you. To try and convince you to get that chip off your shoulder you've been carrying around for almost ten years but has gotten most noticeable the last two weeks."

Ramsey rubbed his hands down his face. He could imagine which one of his relatives had called Dillon. It could have been any one of them. He hadn't been in the best of moods and they all knew it. And they had no idea as to why.

"I don't need this, Dillon."

"Okay, but can I ask you one thing?"

"Yes."

"Do you love her?"

The question, to Ramsey's way of thinking, came out of the blue. It was one he definitely hadn't expected. But with Dillon he would be honest because even now, his very heart, every part of his body, knew the true answer.

"Yes, I love her."

Dillon was silent for a moment and then he said, "She might have set out to deceive you. However, you did admit that she wanted to confess all, but you talked her out of saying anything."

"Yes, but only because I assumed she wanted to talk about something else."

"Does it matter? I can't help but remember the woman who for two solid weeks got up before five o'clock every morning and cooked two meals a day for your men. She befriended them. And when you think about it, she really could have left you in a bind. Even you admitted the guys worked harder while she was there and that they broke all kinds of shearing records."

Ramsey threw his head back. "Is there a point you're trying to make, Dillon?"

"Just a suggestion."

"Which is?" Ramsey said in a hard tone.

"Basically the same one you gave me a few months back. You were the one who told me that in some things you need to know when and how to adjust your thinking, to be flexible. Especially if it's a woman you want."

"I don't want, Chloe. At least not in my life."

"You're absolutely sure about that?"

Ramsey knew that, but now, he wasn't sure. When it came

to Chloe, the woman still had him tied in knots. And he wasn't sure about anything, other than the fact that he still loved her.

He pulled in a deep breath. The truth of the matter was that he hadn't been able to adjust his thinking when it came to Chloe. It had been a while since he'd had a woman in his life and over the years he'd gotten pretty set in his ways. But what Dillon said was right. She hadn't had to hang around preparing those meals for his men for two weeks. She could have bailed after the first day. But she hadn't.

She had told him that she loved him, but he'd never told her that he loved her as well. Instead he had asked her to leave. What if she'd left town? Suddenly he didn't want to think about that possibility.

But he did. He thought about it a lot. He was still thinking about it later that evening when he and Callum got together to shoot a game of pool over at one of the local pool halls they frequented. The thought that if she were to leave Denver he would not be able to find her grated on his mind. As well as the thought that he needed to let her know that he had appreciated what she'd done for two weeks, feeding his men good food, letting them know they were appreciated. She had gone out of her way to put a little sunshine in their days.

All right, he would be the first to admit he probably did still carry around that chip on his shoulder that might have caused him to overreact. After all, she had tried telling him something that day, but he hadn't wanted to hear anything she'd had to say, fearing the worst and not wanting to deal with it. And although her original intentions might not have been honorable, she had stayed around, hung in and made a difference.

His thoughts shifted back to the possibility that she had not remained in Denver. Not being able to take not knowing any longer, he turned and handed his pool cue to Callum. "I'm going after her."

Callum accepted the cue stick and merely rolled his eyes. "About time."

Ramsey raised a brow. "And you think you can talk?"

Callum gave him a sly smile. "Yes, now that I've made up my mind about something."

Ramsey would have taken the time to inquire just what that *something* was had he not been so eager to head out the door.

Chloe pushed away from her desk and glanced out the window. It was hard to believe it had been three weeks since she had left Ramsey's ranch. Three solid weeks and this morning her suspicions had been confirmed. She was pregnant.

If she thought hard enough she figured there were a number of times they had gotten careless, like one of those times in the shower. But it really didn't matter when it happened, the fact remained that it had happened. Now she had to decide whether she would tell him before returning to Florida. He had a right to know, but whether she would tell him now or later, she just wasn't sure.

She had had lunch with Ramsey's sisters last week. Evidently, he was in rare form and they figured his less-than-desirable attitude lately had had something to do with her. Chloe was surprised he hadn't told them the entire story and fighting back tears she'd ended up telling them everything. How she had initially deceived him and then fell in love with him. Instead of taking their brother's side as she had figured they would do, they ended up crying right along with her. They were convinced she loved Ramsey and that it was a shame he couldn't see it for himself. They were convinced once he thought things through he would see the truth for himself. If only she could believe that.

Chloe stood and walked over to the window to continue to look out. Her work here in Denver was finished and Lucia would be handling things from here on out. Her east coast staff was presently looking for a new prospect for the October issue of *Simply Irresistible,* and that was fine with her. She was ready to move on.

Going back to her desk, she picked up her cell phone to call Lucia who had left that morning for Atlanta to sit in on a leadership workshop with a few of Chloe's other employees. She got Lucia's answering machine. "Lou, I'm not feeling well, so I'm going to leave early for your place. That's where I'll be if you need me for anything. Otherwise, I'll see you tomorrow when you return."

Feeling tired and sleepy, Chloe took a long nap as soon as she got home. When she awoke, she saw it had gotten dark outside and she felt hungry. Reminding herself that although her pregnancy was in the very early stages, that whenever she ate she was eating for two, she went into the kitchen and prepared a meal.

Hours later she had showered, changed into her favorite yellow sundress and had grabbed a book to read when the doorbell sounded. Chloe went to the door and glanced through the peephole. Her breath caught in her chest and she pressed a hand to her throat. Standing on Lucia's front porch was the man who'd captured her heart, the father of the baby she carried in her womb. Ramsey Westmoreland.

When Chloe opened the door, Ramsey could only stand there and stare at her. At that moment he thought the same thing he had that first morning he'd seen her: She was beautiful.

He did recall that morning. He remembered how he'd tried getting away from her once he saw how attracted he'd been to her. That was something that had not been her fault. And he had done something that morning so unlike him. He had raced off in his truck, leaving his front door open to a stranger. He had assumed she was the cook and he hadn't given her time to state otherwise.

Once he'd knocked the chip off his shoulder and had taken the time to analyze the situation, sort out the mess, he saw he had contributed to the misunderstanding. She was right in saying that although her original plans may not have been honorable, she had hung around and helped him out. He could just imagine how things would have turned out if she hadn't.

"Ramsey, what are you doing here?"

Her question brought his attention back to the present. "I'd like to talk to you, if at all possible."

He saw the wary look in her eyes before she nodded, opened the door wider and then moved aside.

When he passed her the first thing Chloe thought was that Ramsey certainly smelled good. And he looked good, too. He was wearing a pair of jeans, a western shirt and boots. He had removed the Stetson from his head once he'd entered the house.

Not asking him to sit, she turned to him. "What do you want to talk about?"

"I owe you an apology. You did try to level with me that day and I stopped you from doing so. Actually, I was afraid to let you."

Chloe lifted a brow. "Why?"

"If you recall, it was the same day my three sisters came to visit and I, of all people, know how overwhelming they can be. I thought that perhaps they may have tried boxing you into a corner about a relationship with me. I haven't been involved with a woman in a while and was afraid you might have begun feeling forced into a situation you weren't quite ready for, and I didn't want to hear you say it. Especially after I'd made plans to ask you to continue a relationship with me once your time was up at the ranch."

Chloe's reaction to his words was a total surprise. "You wanted to continue a relationship with me?"

She saw the intensity in his eyes when he said, "Yes."

Happiness swirled in her veins and the intensity was back in his eyes. But still…

She searched his face. "Why, Ramsey? Why did you want to continue a relationship with me?"

He didn't say anything for a moment, but the look on his features basically said it all. There were emotions there she hadn't seen before, emotions he'd never revealed to her until now. But still, she needed to hear him say the words.

He must have known what she needed. Placing his hat on the rack, he then walked the few feet over to her to stand in front of her. She sucked in a deep breath and lifted her face to meet his gaze when he did so.

"The reason I wanted to continue a relationship with you, Chloe, is because I had fallen in love with you."

He reached out and took her hand in his. "I know for us to be in love is not a cure-all. But at least it's a start and is more than most people have. I do love you, Chloe, and I want for us to be together. I don't want it to sound like I'm rushing things, but I want to marry you. I want to give you my babies one day. Bring you to the ranch to live with me as my wife. But

I know those have to be the things you want. I'm not asking you to give up anything for me, for our love. When you have to go away and travel for your magazine company, I'll modify my schedule to travel with you. I—"

Chloe held up her finger and placed it on his lips. "If nothing else, these past two weeks have shown me I have people capable of managing the magazine without me. Besides, I rather like the idea of living on your ranch, being your wife and the mother of your babies."

The brilliance of his smile touched her. "So you will marry me?"

"Yes."

"And if you want, we can have a long engagement," he said pulling her into his arms.

Chloe chuckled, shaking her head. "Now there's the kicker. A long engagement might not work for us, unfortunately."

He lifted a brow. "Not that I'm complaining, but why wouldn't it work?"

She paused and then she reached out and took his hand in hers and carried it to her stomach. "Already, your baby is here," she said in a whisper.

Chloe thought the look on his face at that moment was priceless. His mouth dropped open in shock. "You're pregnant."

She threw her head back and laughed. "No, *we're* pregnant."

Filled with more joy that he could stand, Ramsey didn't care how such a thing could have happened when they had used protection. It didn't matter. He wanted their baby. He pulled her closer into his arms and captured her mouth with his. The kiss was hungry, it was intense and, Chloe thought, it was full of love.

When he released her, he wrapped his arms tightly around her waist. "We're getting married as soon as it can be arranged."

She looked up at him. "We don't really have to, you know. Women have babies out of wedlock all the time and—"

"My child will be born a Westmoreland."

She chuckled. "If that's what you want."

"That's what I want. Will you go back to the ranch with me tonight so we can make plans?"

She lifted her brow. "Is that the only thing we'll make when we get there?"

Now it was Ramsey's turn to smile. He answered honestly, "No."

Chloe wrapped her arms around Ramsey's neck. "Um, I didn't think so."

When Ramsey bent his head to hers, she was ready and knew that this was just the beginning.

Epilogue

No one had asked why Ramsey and Chloe wanted a rather quick wedding. They were just happy to see Ramsey finally tying the knot. It was a beautiful day in May and all the Westmorelands came.

Chloe was overwhelmed at the huge family she'd married into. And there were several celebrities—national motorcycle superstar Thorn Westmoreland, well-known author Stone Westmoreland (a.k.a. Rock Mason), and Princess Delaney Westmoreland Yasir, wife of Sheikh Jamal Ari Yasir. Everyone welcomed her into the family with open arms. She couldn't help but smile, thinking it was a small world in that her father had already met the young, up-and-coming Senator Reginald Westmoreland at a fundraiser for a Georgia congressman last year. And Chloe was practically beaming in delight that Ramsey had also told her a few weeks ago that he would pose for the cover of her magazine.

Deciding they didn't want a huge wedding, Chloe had worn a beautiful tailored white pantsuit and with Ramsey by her side they walked around Shady Tree Ranch, where the beautiful outdoor wedding had taken place, greeting their guests. She got a chance to talk to one of Ramsey's elderly relatives, James Westmoreland. He was the one responsible for bringing the Atlanta and Denver Westmorelands together.

Chloe enjoyed talking to James and after talking with him she knew most of the story about Raphael and the mystery about the man's life that was yet to be solved.

A short while later, Ramsey took Chloe's hand in his and led her away from their guests. Even his men had come to the wedding and had brought their wives. She thought they looked good in their Sunday best.

"So, we don't know if those women were wives of Raphael or not." She noticed Ramsey was leading her farther and farther away from their guests.

Ramsey threw his head back and laughed. "I can only vouch for one of them and that's my great-grandmother Gemma. I know they got married because we have a copy of their marriage certificate. The others...we shall see."

"Is there anyone else besides Dillon even interested in finding out?"

"Yes, Megan. But she plans to do things differently. Unlike Dillon, she doesn't want to do the research herself but plans to hire a private detective to solve the mystery for her."

Ramsey stopped walking and turned to her. "I didn't bring you out here to talk about Raphael."

Chloe glanced around and saw they were a distance from the house. "And why did you bring me out here?"

He pulled her into his arms. "To say in private what I said in front of everyone today. I love you, sweetheart, and for the

rest of my life I promise to show you just how much, and I
will love and honor you always."

Tears sprang into Chloe's eyes. "And I love you."

The moment Ramsey had pulled her into his arms, Chloe
knew that their lives would be filled with love, passion and
plenty of hot Westmoreland nights.

* * * * *

Don't miss the next Westmorelands' romance from
New York Times *bestselling author Brenda Jackson*
on sale September 14, 2010
from Silhouette Desire

Aella closed her eyes and sensed a distinct shift, like movement from the world around her to the unseen world.

She opened her eyes. And had a slight shock at the man standing ten feet away. He wasn't just any man. Her heart leaped and pounded. He reminded her of a fierce warrior from an ancient civilization. Incan? She wasn't sure but she felt his deep power and masculinity.

I'm Aella. Are you the guardian of this sacred site? she asked, hoping her telepathy was strong.

Fox's entire body soared with joy. Fox struggled to put his personal pleasure aside.

Greetings, Aella. I'm the assistant guardian to this sacred area. You may call me Fox. How can I be of service to you, Aella? he asked.

I'm searching for a green sphere. A legend says that the Emperor Pachacuti had seven emerald spheres created for the Emerald Key necklace. He had seven of his priestesses and priests travel the world to hide these spheres from evil forces. It is said that when all seven spheres are found, restrung and worn, that Light will return to the Earth. The fourth sphere is here, at your sacred site. Are you aware of it? Aella held her breath. She loved looking at him, especially his sensual mouth. The desire to kiss him came out of nowhere.

Fox was stunned by the request. *I know of the Emerald*

Key necklace because I served the emperor at the time it was created. However, I did not realize that one of the spheres is here.

Aella felt sad. Why? Every time she looked at Fox, her heart felt as if it would tear out of her chest. *May I stay in touch with you as I work with this site?* she asked.

Of course. Fox wanted nothing more than to be here with her. To absorb her ephemeral beauty and hear her speak once more.

Aella's spirit lifted. What *was* this strange connection between them? Her curiosity was strong, but she had more pressing matters. In the next few days, Aella knew her life would change forever. How, she had no idea....

*Look for REUNION
by USA TODAY bestselling author Lindsay McKenna,
available April 2010, only from Silhouette® Nocturne™.*

HARLEQUIN® Romance®

ROMANCE, RIVALRY
AND A FAMILY REUNITED

THE BRIDES of BELLA ROSA

William Valentine and his beloved wife, Lucia, live
a beautiful life together, but when his former love Rosa
and the secret family they had together resurface,
an instant rivalry is formed. Can these families
get through the past and come together as one?

*Step into the world of Bella Rosa
beginning this April with*

Beauty and the Reclusive Prince
by
RAYE MORGAN

Eight volumes to collect and treasure!

SPECIAL EDITION

**INTRODUCING A BRAND-NEW MINISERIES
FROM *USA TODAY* BESTSELLING AUTHOR**

KASEY MICHAELS

SECOND-CHANCE BRIDAL

At twenty-eight, widowed single mother
Elizabeth Carstairs thinks she's left love behind
forever....until she meets Will Hollingsbrook.
Her sons' new baseball coach is the handsomest
man she's ever seen—and the more time they
spend together, the more undeniable the
connection between them. But can Elizabeth
leave the past behind and open her heart to
a second chance at love?

FIND OUT IN
SUDDENLY A BRIDE

*Available in April
wherever books are sold.*

REQUEST YOUR FREE BOOKS!

2 FREE NOVELS
PLUS 2
FREE GIFTS!

Passionate, Powerful, Provocative!

YES! Please send me 2 FREE Silhouette Desire® novels and my 2 FREE gifts (gifts are worth about $10). After receiving them, if I don't wish to receive any more books, I can return the shipping statement marked "cancel." If I don't cancel, I will receive 6 brand-new novels every month and be billed just $4.05 per book in the U.S. or $4.74 per book in Canada. That's a saving of almost 15% off the cover price! It's quite a bargain! Shipping and handling is just 50¢ per book in the U.S. and 75¢ per book in Canada.* I understand that accepting the 2 free books and gifts places me under no obligation to buy anything. I can always return a shipment and cancel at any time. Even if I never buy another book, the two free books and gifts are mine to keep forever.

225 SDN E39X   326 SDN E4AA

Name _____ (PLEASE PRINT) _____

Address _____ Apt. # _____

City _____ State/Prov. _____ Zip/Postal Code _____

Signature (if under 18, a parent or guardian must sign) _____

Mail to the Silhouette Reader Service:
IN U.S.A.: P.O. Box 1867, Buffalo, NY 14240-1867
IN CANADA: P.O. Box 609, Fort Erie, Ontario L2A 5X3
Not valid for current subscribers to Silhouette Desire books.

Want to try two free books from another line?
Call 1-800-873-8635 or visit www.morefreebooks.com.

* Terms and prices subject to change without notice. Prices do not include applicable taxes. N.Y. residents add applicable sales tax. Canadian residents will be charged applicable provincial taxes and GST. Offer not valid in Quebec. This offer is limited to one order per household. All orders subject to approval. Credit or debit balances in a customer's account(s) may be offset by any other outstanding balance owed by or to the customer. Please allow 4 to 6 weeks for delivery. Offer available while quantities last.

Your Privacy: Silhouette Books is committed to protecting your privacy. Our Privacy Policy is available online at www.eHarlequin.com or upon request from the Reader Service. From time to time we make our lists of customers available to reputable third parties who may have a product or service of interest to you. If you would prefer we not share your name and address, please check here. ☐

Help us get it right—We strive for accurate, respectful and relevant communications. To clarify or modify your communication preferences, visit us at www.ReaderService.com/consumerchoice.

SDES10